THE MANY ADVENTURES OF PENGEY PENGUIN

THE MANY ADVENTURES OF PENGEY PENGUIN

by

John Burns

Illustrations

by

James Coles

THE MANY ADVENTURES OF PENGEY PENGUIN

Text copyright © 2005 by John Burns

Illustrations copyright © 2005 John Burns

For information contact: San Francisco Story Works, 386 Union Street, San Francisco, California 94133

Printed in The United States of America

First Edition

ISBN 0-9774227-0-4

SAN:>>>>>>>>> 257-5248 <<<<<<<<<

Library of Congress Cataloging-in-Publication data on file.

™ 2005 Pengey Penguin
United States Patent and Trademark Authority

Published by San Francisco Story Works
San Francisco, California

Contents

Lovingly Edited

by

Judy Weiss

Acknowledgments

I have so many people to thank for this little book. Judith McCarthy for being my constant reader and friend, Jim Berry and his assistant Carolyn George, Travis Rivers without whose help deadlines might never have been met, Marie-Ann Widrig for expert digital completion, my daughters Lauren and Maggie for keeping the child alive in me, and Carol Jean, my amazing wife, my cheerleader, and the most wonderful person in my world.

Preface

Somewhere in the Land of Legends, a magical place situated between the stardust memories of the Milky Way and the emerald lands at the end of the rainbow, there lives a very small, very curious, and very clever little emperor penguin.

His name is Pengey Penguin.

Even though he was abandoned under most unusual circumstances, he grew to be an adventurous spirit, undaunted by his troubles and driven by unwavering devotion to his principles and the love of Wendy, the human who saved him from certain death by starvation.

Now it should be thoroughly understood that Pengey is not very tall and he is certainly not very strong, but he is very quick, extremely smart, exceedingly polite, and very well mannered.

This is his story or, at least, how it all began.

He already likes you, and it's his greatest wish that you'll like him, all his friends, and his bedtime story, too.

—J. B.

Chapter 1

The Departure

Once upon a time a mother penguin named Beatrice was preparing for her trip back to the sea. She had just given birth to the egg that she and her husband, Fred, named "Pengey". It was time for her to leave the penguin colony in search of the food that would nourish her back to health, so she could return to Fred and their beautiful egg some two months later.

It was very sad for Fred and Beatrice to say good-bye. They knew of the perils of the deep ocean where she would forage for food. While she was away she would need to eat and eat until she was quite fat and plump in order to nurture Pengey once he was hatched from his eggshell.

Beatrice and Fred said good-bye. They craned their necks in graceful arcs and rubbed their beaks together for what might be the last time. For they both knew of the dangers of leopard seals and orca whales and sharks that would eat a penguin if given the slightest chance.

With her last wave to Fred, Beatrice turned away and trundled off toward the ocean.

It was an extremely long walk to the water because, you see, when Beatrice first made her egg the ice floe between ocean and land was quite narrow. But since then winter had set in, and the normally cold and harsh temperature in Antarctica had become even more severe, making the ice sheet over fifty miles wide where she and Fred had settled with their colony.

Beatrice had plenty of company on her walk because all the other mom Penguins were also returning to the sea. Each had the same task at hand. So the procession of over two thousand mother penguins marched off to the sea.

Beatrice was a very fine-looking penguin, and she had quite the pleasingly plump little belly. So whenever she came to a hill in the snow-covered land, she would simply lie on her tummy, push with her feet, and slide all the way to the bottom.

Now to many this might not seem such a great trick, but when you have very short legs and have to walk over fifty miles in freezing cold, wind-blown weather it's a good idea to make the trip as easy as possible. Besides, it's fun to slide down the hills.

Many days later, Beatrice came to where the ocean meets the icy shores of Antarctica. She was happy because she would soon eat fresh fish. She was very hungry from her long stay inland. She had not eaten in over two months, and the prospect of the fresh krill and tasty little fish made her jump for joy.

Before Beatrice plunged into the ocean, she turned back and called out a loud cry to Fred and Pengey. She knew that her cry would not carry over the fifty miles. She did it as a symbolic gesture so they might not worry too much.

Without making another sound, Beatrice jumped headlong into the icy waters. The cold water felt good to Beatrice because, like all penguins, she had a thick layer of fat and waterproof feathers to keep her warm even in the coldest water.

Beatrice was also like most other penguins in that she could divert her blood flow away from her skin, and therefore she was almost completely immune to cold. This characteristic also enabled her to hold her breath for an extremely long time.

Beatrice was a very fast swimmer indeed. And within a few moments she had caught and gobbled up her first batch of krill. The tiny crustaceans contain lots of vitamins and nutrients that are good for penguins.

And so it went for Beatrice as she carried on gathering food and getting plump for the long walk across the floe and back to Fred and Pengey some two months later.

Chapter 2

DAD AND PENGEY

Meanwhile back at the floe, Fred was balancing Pengey's egg on his feet and keeping it snuggled safely in his brood pouch.

Winter was surely here, and the days now only held a couple of minutes of sunshine. Fred was a proud dad, as were all the other father penguins.

To wile away the time and to pass on the things a dad thought essential to his egg, Fred would sing songs and tell stories to Pengey—songs and stories about his youth as a single penguin when he was traveling the world. He told of how he met Beatrice and fell in love with her.

He told Pengey about all his zany friends, even about the ones who were not so nice, and about those who went on to become very famous penguins. And so it was on the ice sheet during the ancient and frigid-cold Dance of the Penguins.

Now for those of you who may not know about this so-called dance, I have to tell you, here and now, that it is surely one of the strangest dances in the world.

For, you see, as the winter days grow shorter, those days become completely deprived of the sun's warming rays. The entire continent is blanketed in darkness, like midnight, twenty-four hours a day. The father penguins have to hover very close together. It is only through sharing their body heat that they manage to survive in the sub zero temperatures. As if the harsh temperatures weren't enough, there is also nothing for them to eat.

They must keep their eggs from falling onto the ice because even a few short moments of that terrible cold will freeze the baby penguin egg to death.

So the dad penguins parade around and take turns standing in the middle of their big circle of friends and relatives. And because there are over two thousand dads in the circle, it is very toasty warm in the middle.

The dance proceeds twenty-four hours a day, all winter long. They cannot stop moving because they would surely freeze if they did.

On and on they go through the darkest and bleakest part of winter until, some nine weeks later, a new springtime and the first rays of sun arrive. The sun breaks through the interminable darkness and spreads it's warming rays on our little colony of penguins.

Fred and all the dad penguins were very happy at this time, not only because of the new warmth, but also because they knew that their mates would soon be back at the colony. And with them they would bring the food to feed the young, just-hatched penguin chicks.

The baby penguins hadn't begun to grow much just yet. So they had to stay on top of their dad's feet and under his brood pouch to stay safe from the cold.

Pengey was a very curious baby penguin, and as soon as he could, he started peeking out from under Fred's tummy feathers to see what was going on. It was all quite fascinating to him.

Fred, of course, was very proud of his curious youngster, who had already started to exhibit amazing athletic abilities. Pengey exercised with great vigor indeed. Flipper stretching and flapping was an exercise in which he excelled. Naturally, Fred showed Pengey many techniques, and naturally Pengey followed his examples to a T.

Some of the mom penguins returned and started to feed their chicks. Day after day came and went and the air got warmer and warmer, but Pengey's mom did not return. Fred knew she was the best swimmer, but still he worried that something might have happened to his lovely Beatrice.

Still more days passed, and most of the other penguin moms had returned to the colony. Their babies began to get big and fat from all the fresh food their moms had brought back with them from the sea.

Most of the other dad penguins left their babies in the care of their mates, and they themselves returned to the sea to find food. They had not eaten in over four months, and many of those dads were very close to starvation.

More lonely and hungry days and nights went by, and the other penguin chicks were getting fatter and fatter, but not Pengey. He had only the nourishment that his dad could provide, and that was very little because Fred himself hadn't had any food in over four months.

Soon Fred knew he would have to leave Pengey if his lovely Beatrice did not return.

At last came that fateful day when Fred could stand it no longer. He knew he was dying of hunger. In order to save himself he would have to abandon little Pengey on the ice sheet in order to search for food. He had stayed a month longer than any of the other dads, and he'd lost over 60 percent of his body weight.

Fred was very weak and at the point of total exhaustion. "I'll be back, Pengey," he said. "As soon as I can catch us some food, I'll be back."

Fred knew only too well what would happen to Pengey. He said, "Be smart and be strong, young penguin. Remember what I've taught you, and hide among the others until I get back."

Pengey cooed longingly, held back his tears, and said bravely, "I understand, Dad."

Fred grabbed Pengey in his flippers and said, in a very determined fashion, "You stay alive. No matter what it takes, you stay alive. I promise I will find you as soon as I can. I will be back."

Fred was grief stricken. Pengey was far too young to be left alone. He turned reluctantly and started to stumble away. He didn't have very far to go, only a couple of miles, because the warm sun of springtime had melted the floe to a small island of ice.

Still, as Pengey watched him go, he thought sadly that his dad looked so weak and exhausted he wondered if he would ever see him again.

Fred looked back one last time at Pengey, waved a tearful good-bye, and staggered toward the ocean. Pengey bowed his head and solemnly recited the Penguin's Prayer for his dad's safe return.

He waved good-bye until his dad was long gone from sight.

Now little Pengey had only his tiny gray pinfeathers to keep him warm. He was very small because he'd had very little to eat in the month since he had hatched from his eggshell. All the other baby penguins were getting tall and fat, but they would not let Pengey have any of their moms' food. In fact, the mother penguins chased Pengey away.

He was now all alone on the ice floe, there was nothing to eat, and there was a terrible storm coming up.

Pengey sat very still and pondered his options. He would have to learn how to swim. But he was too little, and the water felt too cold to him. Pengey was very confused and very hungry, so he sat down on the snow next to a big brown rock.

He knew that he had to get into the safety of the big circle of penguins. So, with great determination, he ran with all his might to the middle of the circle, and hid in and among the others. They chased him away, but he ran fast and evaded their shoving and pushing. He was afraid, but at least he was warm.

When nighttime fell, at the end of his first day alone, the older penguins just forgot he was there, and so Pengey stayed toasty warm stuffed in the middle of the colony.

Chapter 3

ADRIFT AT SEA

The huge storm blew in over the ice floe. The hurricane-force winds blew mightily all through the night and all the rest of the next day. When it was over, the floe had split in two, and the larger part with most of the other penguin moms and babies stayed firmly attached to the glacier.

Pengey's floe had become a tiny island of ice, just barely over thirty feet across. The sun shown warm and bright, and Pengey sat in the middle of the floe with a rather bewildered look on his face.

He was holding on to the big brown rock with his flippers. He thought, "Wow! If I hadn't been holding on to this rock, the wind would have pushed me into the sea. And the sea would have gobbled me up."

Pengey was alone, to be sure, but on the floe, all around him, were little anchovies that the sea had washed up onto the ice. It was hard for little Pengey to eat a whole fish, even ones as small as these were. But he chomped down with his little beak and ate one. It tasted kind of funny at first, but it didn't make him sick, so he ate another and then another until he was filled to the tippity top.

The day was getting warmer, and the fish were scattered all about his little floe. So Pengey decided to gather up all the anchovies and put them in one spot.

It took him all day, but by the time the sun was setting and it was nighttime Pengey had over one hundred anchovies stacked up in neat little rows. He covered them with snow to keep them fresh, and that's what Pengey ate for the next ten days.

It was also most fortunate that it was sunny and warm during those days so the big brown rock could absorb lots of heat. Pengey could cover himself with snow and snuggle next to the rock at night and not freeze to death. During those long days, when nighttime fell, he went to sleep very, very lonely, but his tummy was full.

Pengey grew a little during those ten days, too. He put on some much-needed weight, and some of his down feathers fell out. Still, he was still quite short—ten inches tall to be exact.

At last it seemed he was starting to look like a real penguin. The crown of his head was all black feathers, and his cheek feathers were white with a slight blush of yellow and orange. He was beginning to feel like quite a proper emperor penguin.

But Pengey's good fortune was starting to dissipate. The anchovies were also ten days old, and as hungry as he was, they were too old to eat. He was getting desperate, and so he walked to the edge of the floe and looked down into the icy blue water. He could see many small fish swimming around eating krill. But with only a small portion of his feathers being waterproof, the water still felt far too cold for swimming.

Another thing that Pengey could not have foreseen was that the ice floe was getting smaller and smaller by the hour. Even the big brown rock that had protected him from the mighty storm was beginning to slip into the sea.

The sun was out more than four hours a day now, and it was getting too hot for a little Penguin who really liked the colder weather. As the sun set on his tenth day on the tiny floe, Pengey wondered what to do. He pondered his options. But no clear ideas came to him by the time he drifted off into a troubled sleep.

The very next morning Pengey awoke with his tummy aching from hunger. The ice floe was now only about the size of a small child's bed. He watched as the big brown rock slipped quietly into the sea. There was nothing left to eat.

Off in the near distance Pengey could see a larger ice floe. He wondered if he could swim to it without freezing in the icy cold water. As he pondered his options, a dark shadow loomed high above his head. Pengey had never seen anything like it. It looked kind of like a penguin, but it was brownish white, it had a big orange beak, and it could fly.

Pengey thought this flying creature might be a friend. He didn't know it was an albatross, a mortal enemy of all baby penguins.

Pengey called out in a long cooing with his tiny voice. He jumped up and down and waved and waved to the albatross. And without any warning, the creature descended onto the ice floe and immediately attacked Pengey.

Now Pengey might not have been very skilled at protecting himself—he wasn't very tall and he was certainly not very strong—but he was exceptionally fast. So he dashed about on the very small ice floe. The big clumsy albatross jumped around and hopped about but could not catch the littlest penguin.

The albatross however, was older and smarter. He fell over and pretended he was hurt and yelled out in pain. Pengey didn't know what to do, but he thought he should help.

The evil albatross's trap worked perfectly, and as soon as Pengey was within striking distance he pounced on him.

Pengey struggled to keep away from the snapping beak of the giant bird that was surely trying to eat him.

Miraculously, Pengey zigged just as the albatross zagged. The albatross lost his hold on Pengey, and Pengey fell off the floe into the deep blue waters of the Antarctic Ocean. He dove as deep as he could and narrowly escaped the crushing beak of the giant bird.

Pengey was cold but not as cold as he thought he might be. He was quite pleased to find out that he could hold his breath for a long time. And so he swam as fast as his little flippers could go toward the larger ice floe.

When Pengey popped his head out of the water, he did not see the albatross anywhere around. And so he breathed a silent and rather chilly sigh of relief.

Chapter 4

THE HUNTING GROUNDS

The huge ice floe now loomed in front of Pengey. It was extremely tall, which made it seem insurmountable for a little penguin. Repeated attempts to get onto it proved it to be exceedingly slippery and made it more than just a little difficult for Pengey to get out of the water.

Pengey was beginning to feel that if he didn't get out of the water pretty soon he would surely freeze to death. He swam all around trying to find a better place to hop onto the floe, but to no avail.

Finally he remembered a story his dad told him about his older cousin Binkey the Rock Hopper Penguin. Binkey would swim as fast as he could toward the shore of an ice floe, pop out of the water at the very last moment, and hop onto the ice. That seemed a very good idea, so Pengey tried it. But it seemed that the icy shores were just too tall for a little penguin like him.

Pengey was near exhaustion, and that is a very bad thing in deep water. He felt that he could not swim another stroke. And then something swam by, something very large.

When Pengey looked for whatever it was, it was gone—vanished into the dark water beneath him. He had a bad feeling about this mysterious thing of the deep; after all, an albatross had just tried to eat him.

So Pengey stayed very still and looked all around him and even into the deep water. As he looked deeper into the water he saw a black speck rapidly advancing and getting larger and larger. It was directly under him and was approaching at terrifying speed.

Pengey swam with all his might toward the shore and narrowly escaped the crushing jaws of a giant leopard seal. The monster seal lunged savagely at little Pengey again and again. But Pengey was the faster swimmer, and he escaped. He was exhausted to be sure. He needed to muster all of his strength for a final assault on the shoreline. But where would he find that strength?

There was no time to think because the leopard seal was only inches away, coming straight at him. If Pengey was going to escape, he had to use all the strength he had and he had to use it now.

He swam as fast as he could, his little flippers pounding and splashing against the relentless ocean waves. The giant seal lunged up behind Pengey with his hideous mouth wide open and his awful teeth snapping.

Pengey remembered Binkey, and at the very last moment he leaped for the shore. He flew through the air and landed on his feet at the very edge of the ice. He teetered back and forth, and his little flippers windmilled around in an effort to keep his balance.

He slipped and slid and was about to fall back into the water when the wave caused by the rushing seal pushed Pengey over the edge and onto the ice floe. The leopard seal crashed into the crags of ice on the shoreline. He banged his head very badly and sank to the bottom of the ocean, never to be seen again.

Pengey scurried across the floe and fell down and rolled around on the soft carpet of snow that was so dry it quickly absorbed all the water from his feathers so he did not freeze to death. He huffed and puffed to catch his breath while the sun's warming rays did their best to take the chill out of his tired little bones.

Off in the distance, Pengey could see some strange-looking, square rock-like things. They were not made of ice or snow but were brown and green in color. There were tall creatures walking around them.

Pengey thought that maybe these creatures were some sort of distant relative—some sort of penguin. Whatever they were, they walked on two feet and seemed to wave their flippers around a lot.

He noted that the feathers of these tall creatures were not very formal. And although Pengey was affronted by this casual manner of dressing, hunger and exhaustion overcame his disapproval. He decided to approach these unusual-looking penguins and ask them for some food.

Chapter 5

THE SIGHTING

Pengey staggered to his feet. He was extremely tired and so hungry that walking was all but impossible. Somehow he managed to trundle off toward the funny-looking brown and green rocks and the tall penguins with the multicolored feathers. "Surely," he thought as he wiped his brow, "they will have some food."

It turned out that the rocks were a lot farther away than they looked. Perhaps it was a condition of the atmosphere or maybe it was an optical illusion, but for whatever reason, the farther Pengey trudged across the snow, the farther away the rocks seemed to be.

Pengey stopped at the crest of a snow-covered hill and looked at them again. They looked a little bigger now. So he lay down on his tummy and tried to slide down the hill the way his dad had shown him.

But it was no use. He didn't weigh enough, and his tummy was simply not big enough to accommodate sliding of any kind, let alone all the way to the bottom of the hill. He struggled back to his weary little feet and continued on.

It was getting dark by now, and Pengey noticed that the creatures were going *inside* the strange brown rocks. He noticed that even though the sun had gone down behind the glacier, it still seemed to be shining inside the rocks.

"How very curious indeed," he thought.

Pengey trudged onward, falling over and over again in complete exhaustion. But the brave little penguin forced himself to get up and trundled closer and closer to the strange creatures and their rock-like homes.

He was pretty close now, so close that Pengey could hear them, but they didn't make sounds like penguins, they made different sounds. It was a language that Pengey didn't recognize. He didn't understand what they were saying, but one thing he did recognize was their laughter.

It didn't sound exactly the same as when penguins laugh, but it felt the same. The laughter and all their talking kept Pengey going. By the time it was nine o'clock at night it was very dark and very quiet, but Pengey had arrived at his destination.

Chapter 6

WENDY

It was so quiet and still that Pengey was beside himself with worry over how to properly introduce himself. After all, he did not know these penguins, and being of good penguin stock himself, he was very much concerned about proper etiquette in these matters.

Although he was quite dizzy and faint from his hunger and exhaustion, he made a simple decision. He would politely knock on the dwellings wherein the sun was still shining, near one of the openings that the tall penguins used to go in and out.

Pengey straightened his feathers as best he could and gently tapped on the entry with his beak. He waited and waited but no one answered. Trying not to be rude, Pengey knocked again, but this time with a little more force.

At last a voice from inside said, "There it is again, sounds like someone knocking at the door."

A different voice said, "I'll go see who it is."

Pengey didn't know what all the sounds meant. He was quite sure now that these were not penguins. Maybe they were the humans that his dad had told him about.

He heard someone walking toward the door. He stepped away from the door and waited for it to open. He had his entire speech rehearsed in his mind. He hoped against hope that humans spoke penguin.

Then Pengey saw, through a little window in the door,

the face of a lady human. She wiped some frost off the glass and looked out at Pengey.

He placed his flipper against his tummy and bowed in a very formal fashion, but it seemed the lady human did not see him. He could hear her sweet voice faintly through the door. He didn't know what the sounds meant.

She said, "I can't see anything out there. I guess it's just the wind."

Pengey waved his little flipper again and again, but the lady human didn't see him. It was too much for Pengey, and he swooned away onto the icy snow.

He must have been out for a couple of minutes. When he awoke he was colder than he had ever been. He struggled to his feet and thought that obviously these human penguins would not give him any food, either. Sadly he began to trundle away.

Pengey had walked only a short distance from the building when he was startled by the opening of the very door where he had been lying. Two very large gentlemen and the lady human wandered out onto the snow. Pengey thought if he had not awakened in time he surely would have been crushed by the feet of the large humans. He hid behind a big round barrel-shaped thing and watched them.

The smaller of the gentlemen was named Bob. Pengey figured it out because that's what the other humans called him.

The great big gentleman was called Jasper. He spoke slowly and used his hands and arms to illustrate what he was talking about. They were funny to watch, and Pengey learned a lot by observing him.

The young woman was called Wendy. She was really pretty and soft spoken and seemed to have a calming effect on Bob and Jasper.

Bob said, "It just seems a shame to waste it all." And he turned to Wendy, who smiled at him with her beautiful white teeth.

Wendy said, "I told you not to catch so many." And she turned to Jasper, who looked a little embarrassed.

Jasper said, "It's not my fault that mine was big. It was big enough for all of us. Bob didn't even have to catch any." He stretched his long arms away from his chest and said, "Mine was this big." Then he put his hands closer together and said, "Not little like the little ones Bob caught."

Pengey observed that before long Bob and Jasper were arguing about what they caught, and they were both using their arms and hands to indicate just how big or how little the things were.

Bob would point to himself and assert, "Mine was bigger."

Jasper would wave his arms and point to himself while he cut Bob off, "Not as big as mine."

Finally Wendy spoke out in a clear, intelligent voice, "Guys! I'm freezing. There's no sense in arguing about who caught the biggest fish. The fact is we're flying out of here in the morning, and we can't take the fish with us. So just leave them out here on the snow, and the seagulls will take care of them."

With that Bob nodded silent agreement, then threw something onto the snow. He walked over to Jasper and silently shook hands with him. Then just as somberly, Bob walked back into the building.

Jasper threw something onto the snow, looked at Wendy, and said, "No one back home will ever believe I caught a fish that big."

Wendy patted Jasper on the back with soft reassurance. She smiled at him in a kindly way and said, "I believe you, Jasper." Jasper looked crestfallen, but he smiled at Wendy and trudged back into the building.

Wendy looked around and sighed. She started to walk back into the building when she saw Pengey peek out from behind the barrel. Wendy looked very curiously at Pengey, then she knelt down to get a better look.

Pengey wasn't afraid of Wendy because she seemed kind and warm. So he took a brave step out from behind his hiding place and another shy step toward her.

Wendy said, "Well, what do we have here?"

Pengey bowed and made a cooing noise, and Wendy smiled back at him.

Pengey wanted to impress Wendy with his formal manners and great intelligence, but he was so hungry he kept edging toward the things that were dropped on the snow. They sure smelled like fish.

Wendy kept an eye on Pengey, and Pengey kept an eye on Wendy and edged his way toward the big pile of fish. One of the fish was over three feet long. It was so big Pengey had no idea of how anyone could ever eat the whole thing.

Wendy rose and walked to Pengey and knelt by his side. She spoke with calm assurance, "This fish is about ten times bigger than you, little guy." Pengey slowly shook his head in bewilderment and cooed remorsefully.

Wendy took a Swiss army knife out of her pocket and said, "How about if I cut off a few pieces for you?" And so she did, sitting there in the freezing cold for almost half an hour cutting off little pieces of the giant fish and feeding them to a very, very hungry little Pengey Penguin.

Pengey was very grateful indeed, and he bowed to Wendy most graciously when he was full. He was so full, in fact, that upon rising from his bow, he lost his balance and plopped down on his bottom.

It might have been because he was so tired or maybe because he was so full but Pengey found it extremely amusing to see his feet straight out and almost completely covered by his bulging tummy.

And so Pengey laughed. It was a tiny and silly sounding little laugh, but it delighted Wendy to no end and so she laughed, too.

Wendy said, "You are a very charming Mr. Penguin."

Pengey stood up, brushed the snow off his feathers, and bowed and cooed a thank you to Wendy. She was quite taken by Pengey's formal manners and what seemed to be his astonishing need to communicate.

She stood up and walked back to the building and opened the door. She looked back at Pengey, who was still cooing and bowing his formal bows of thank you. Wendy said to Pengey, "It's nice and warm inside. Do you want to come in?"

Pengey walked to the door, and he felt something he had never felt before, the radiance of heat. He thought that the sun was surely shining inside the building. The sensation was a little frightening, so he backed away and bowed some more, and as he did Pengey looked at Wendy, pointed to himself, and used the same arm movements that Jasper used to describe his big fish.

Pengey looked sincerely into Wendy's eyes, shyly cocked his head, pointed to himself with his flipper, and stretched his flippers out all the way across his chest.

Wendy looked a little confused, but Pengey repeated the gestures over and over in the same shy fashion. It finally dawned on Wendy that Pengey was trying to say "I'm big."

Wendy laughed and knelt in the snow next to Pengey and said, "You're big? Is that what you're trying to say?"

Pengey nodded yes in a very sincere fashion and repeated the gesture.

Wendy tossed her head back and laughed out loud and said, "Why, yes. You most certainly are very big indeed." She smiled again, "Are you sure you won't come in?"

Pengey shook his head no.

Wendy said, "Okay. I guess you know what you're doing. Good night, my little penguin."

Bob came to the door, poked his head out, and yelled, "Hey Wendy, you comin' in? We're closin' it down for the night."

Wendy looked at Bob from her place on the snow and said, "Hey Bob, come here for a second, I want you to meet someone."

Bob walked to where Wendy knelt in the snow. He saw Pengey standing there and said, "Who's that?"

Wendy pointed to Pengey and said, "He's my new friend."

Bob said, "That's got to be the littlest penguin I've ever seen."

Pengey made a gesture with his flippers that looked like, "Excuse me!" And then he repeated the gesture, "I'm big."

Bob said, "What's he trying to say?"

"He's trying to tell you that he's big."

Pengey repeated his gesture with a firm look of resolve.

Bob looked at Wendy and said, "Well, I'll be. He *is* saying, "I'm big." He knelt down beside Wendy, and Pengey bowed in a very formal fashion to Bob, who said, "Sorry little fella. It's just that I couldn't see ya too well from up there."

Pengey walked a couple of steps closer to Bob and

extended his flipper. Bob looked confused and Wendy said, "He wants to shake hands."

Bob touched Pengey's flipper with his finger and his thumb because Pengey's flipper was so little that's all that would fit. They shook vigorously, and Pengey bowed, and so, in turn, Bob bowed to Pengey.

Bob laughed and said, "You're quite the man, aren't you?"

Pengey nodded very seriously, and Bob and Wendy smiled in admiration.

Wendy asked, "Do you have a name?" She pointed to herself and said, "I'm Wendy." She pointed to Bob and said, "His name is Bob." She pointed to herself and said, "Wendy."

Wendy touched her finger to Pengey's chest and said, "You . . . what's your name?"

Pengey got it right away but didn't know how to speak human, so he pointed to himself, spun around in a happy little dance, and pointed to Wendy.

Bob asked Wendy, "What's he trying to say this time?"

Wendy looked curiously at Pengey and tried to figure out what his little dance and all his pointing could possibly mean. She looked at Pengey and asked, "'Penguin'? Is your name 'Penguin'?"

Pengey shook his head no!

Wendy shook her head in dismay and said, "I'm afraid you've got me stumped. So I guess I'll just have to call you 'Pengey.'"

Pengey jumped up and down and cooed very loudly. It was quite obvious to everyone that he was extremely happy.

Wendy asked, "'Pengey'? Is that your name?"

Pengey nodded yes, and he tilted his head and cooed happily.

Bob said, "Well, I'll be."

Wendy looked at Pengey and smiled and said, "Well, it was a pleasure to meet you Mister Pengey Penguin."

Pengey bowed and smiled at Wendy.

And with that Wendy and Bob stood up and walked back toward the building. Wendy waved good night, and Pengey waved back to her. Then Wendy closed the door.

Pengey walked to a place in back of the barrel where the wind became calm. He found a spot where another tiny building with a little smokestack adjoined Wendy's building. It hummed and radiated heat, so he snuggled into the snow next to it.

And so it was on that night that his tummy was full. It was also a little strange that he felt comfortable among these humans. His last thoughts as he fell fast asleep were that humans were pretty cool, and he'd like to get to know them better, a lot better.

He slept well and had really good dreams that were mostly about what it would be like if he had a lot of humans for friends.

Chapter 7

ABANDONED

Morning came quickly, and Pengey was wide awake as the sun rose over the glaciers.

He immediately dashed over to the very big fish and nibbled at it, but it was frozen solid. He picked up some of the tiny shreds that Wendy had dropped the night before, but they were more like icicles and quite impossible to eat.

It wasn't long before the sun was shining inside the buildings again. And shortly afterward came the sound of the humans talking their strange language and the smell of strange things cooking. Smelled pretty good, too. Pengey thought that he might like to try human food one day.

The door opened and Wendy called out, "Pengey? Are you still here?"

Pengey dashed to where Wendy was standing and cooed and bowed a formal, "good morning" salutation.

Wendy said, "Oh! There you are." She made the gesture of putting her hand to her mouth and asked, "Are you hungry? Do you want something to eat?"

Pengey bowed and nodded his head yes, and then he repeated his bow.

Wendy looked at Pengey and said, "You're trying to say 'thank you,' aren't you, Pengey."

Pengey nodded affirmatively.

Wendy turned and disappeared inside. A moment later she opened the door carrying a small blue bowl filled with chopped fish. She knelt down, placed the bowl on the snow in front of her, and stood back up. Pengey looked at the bowl of fish most curiously.

Wendy said, "I want you to know I used the best fish we had in the house."

Pengey bowed but didn't eat the fish.

Wendy said, "It's okay, you can eat it."

But Pengey backed away because he had never seen a bowl before and didn't know what to do with it.

Wendy sat down on the snow, picked a piece of fish out of the bowl, and held it out to Pengey. Pengey approached Wendy, gently took the piece of fish in his beak, and gobbled it down.

She looked at him sadly and said, "I'm going to miss you, little guy."

Pengey smiled and made the gesture, "I'm big," and gobbled down another piece of fish from Wendy's outstretched hand.

She put another piece of fish into his beak and said, "I know you're big, and I want to take care of you, but I'm leaving for New York City in a few minutes."

Pengey had no idea what Wendy was saying, but he sensed the sadness in her voice.

Just then there was a strange, loud humming sound that seemed to be coming toward them very fast. Pengey turned to face the sound and saw something large and silver flying in the sky. It was like a huge albatross, and it was rapidly approaching.

He quickly dashed to Wendy's side and hid under the folds of her coat.

Wendy was surprised that the little penguin was so trusting. She peeked under her coat to see Pengey with his little face buried in his flippers, his whole body quivering in fear. She began to pet Pengey and console him with her soothing voice. "It's just an airplane, Pengey. It's come to take Bob and Jasper and me back to New York so we can finish making our movie."

But Pengey was having none of this explanation, for the loud and prolonged sound of the airplane was upon them as it descended to the snow and landed.

Pengey stayed close to Wendy now, for the roar of the airplane was deafening. She continued to console him as Bob came out through the door. He was surprised to see Wendy sitting on the snow, and so he asked her, "Why in the world are you sitting in the snow? It must be twenty below out here."

Wendy carefully lifted the corner of her coat to reveal Pengey, who was still quivering in fear of the airplane.

Bob stared at Pengey, shook his head, and said, "The little guy's taken a likin' to you, Wendy." Wendy nodded and covered Pengey over with the folds of her coat.

Bob said, "The plane is here."

Wendy said, "Will you get my things? I have to say good-bye to someone."

"I'll be glad to," said Bob, "but we have to take off in two minutes." He walked back into the building. Wendy sat in the snow with Pengey, and the airplane pulled up close to the building with its engines humming away.

Wendy said, "I'm going to miss you, little one, but it's time for me to go. If you ever get to New York City, you'll just have to come and see me." She took Pengey out from under her coat and put him on the snow.

Bob and Jasper walked out of the hut, slipped their backpacks over their shoulders, and approached Wendy. Bob handed Wendy her travel bag and said, "Come on, it's time to go."

Wendy looked at Pengey and said very softly, "I have to go now."

She stood up while Pengey just stood there shaking his head no.

Jasper said, "Why don't we take the little penguin with us?"

"Because he doesn't want to go," said Wendy.

Wendy, Bob, and Jasper walked toward the airplane. Pengey watched them go. He could see strange marks on Wendy's travel bag, marks that spelled out her name, *Wendy Fitzgerald*.

Wendy kept turning around and waving to Pengey, but Pengey was too afraid of the airplane to look. It was all happening too fast. Even as she climbed the last of the stairs into the airplane she waved to him, but Pengey was just too terrified to see.

In the next moment the airplane moved away from the building with a deafening roar from its mighty engines. Pengey looked angrily at the airplane; it wasn't an albatross after all but something even bigger. It was a monster that had come to gobble up Wendy, Bob, and Jasper, and pretty soon they'd all be gone.

He just couldn't understand why they all went so willingly. He thought, "Maybe that's just what humans do."

Pengey was alone with no one to talk to and the noise from the airplane was now so frightening that he ran into the building to escape its thunder. It wasn't very hard to do because Bob had left the door open just enough for Pengey to squeeze through.

The airplane continued to pull slowly away toward the end of the runway.

Chapter 8

THE ALBATROSS AND THE AIRPLANE

Pengey didn't like it inside the building because it was too warm and the noise of the airplane was just as frightening as when he was outside.

He looked around and saw many strange things that he couldn't identify. But after all, he was just a little penguin, and what was he supposed to know about the lives of humans?

When he looked on the wall he saw a picture of Wendy. He knew that he liked her, and he wanted to save her from the awful airplane.

Pengey hopped up onto a box, then onto a chair, and then onto the desktop. He stood close to the picture of Wendy, but it wasn't the same as standing next to her. Sadly he sat down on the desktop and hung his head and pondered his options.

What should he do? The albatross was leaving. It might have already eaten Wendy. There was no time to lose. He had to act now or lose Wendy forever.

There in front of him on the desktop was a small card that had a lot of words on it. Most of the words meant nothing to him, but one of those words spelled *Wendy*. He decided that this card was a way to find her.

Pengey picked the card up in his beak, jumped off the desk, and ran for the open door. He stumbled over a sort of miniature, pretend human. The doll was dressed like a wilderness explorer. One of the things the doll wore was a sack strapped to its back.

Pengey thought that this backpack would be useful, so he put Wendy's card inside it, took the backpack off the pretend human, and dashed for the door.

At last he was outside. The airplane was ready to take off. Pengey looked at the fish in Wendy's blue bowl. He thought, "I'd better take some of this fish just in case Wendy gets hungry after I save her." So he quickly stuffed some of the fish into his backpack, slipped it over his shoulders, and started to run after the plane.

He was not going to let the giant albatross eat his Wendy, or Bob or Jasper, either.

Pengey ran with all his might, past the frozen fish where Wendy had fed him the night before. He ran past Jasper's huge fish and the many seagulls that were arguing and yelling at each other.

Pengey ran as fast as his little legs could carry him toward the airplane. He was sure that Wendy was in that albatross.

He felt strong because had eaten and slept well the night before. He thought he still had a chance to save Wendy, so he ran with a great burst of speed.

The airplane was ready for takeoff, and its motors were revved up to a deafening roar. Pengey ran on fearlessly. The airplane started to move toward Pengey.

A dark shadow suddenly hovered over Pengey, and this time he could not escape the snapping beak of a very real and giant albatross. The huge bird grabbed Pengey by his backpack and hoisted him straight up, up into the air.

Faster and faster the albatross flew Pengey into the sky. He looked at Pengey and laughed an evil laugh, and so the albatross did not see the rapidly approaching airplane. When he looked up, the plane was only inches away.

The albatross dropped Pengey in midair and tried to get out of the way of the gigantic plane, but it bonked the albatross very badly, and he fell down, down, down onto the snow, never to be seen again.

Pengey fell toward the airplane, and the rush of air off the engines pushed the little penguin under the wing. He sailed backward as the airplane took flight. He landed very hard against a big, fat round thing.

The airplane was in the air and gaining altitude when the wheels started to go up into the body of the plane. Pengey was on one of those wheels, hanging on for dear life.

Chapter 9

THE STOWAWAY

The landing gear and its wheels were drawn up and into the body of the airplane. And along with the wheel on the right-hand side, so went Pengey.

Pengey thought he was done for. He thought he had been eaten by the enormous albatross that had eaten Wendy. He lay on the wheel, which was stuffed inside the belly of the airplane, and waited to die. But he did not die. He just sat there wondering when he would die.

After an hour or so Pengey decided that he had had quite enough of this albatross and took it upon himself to find someone to complain to. There was a slight problem in that the wheel was sort of wedged into a socket of sorts, and there was very little room to move about.

Pengey got quite angry indeed, and when he got angry, he pondered his options. He let out a very loud cooing noise just to blow off some steam. He was hungry, too. He thought if it was going to take this long to die, he might as well have a full tummy.

He opened his little backpack and took out a few small pieces of fish. They were still cold and fresh from lying around on the snow, so he gobbled a few of them down.

He was going to eat more, but he decided to save some for later, just in case this dying thing took more time than it had already.

It was pretty dark inside the wheel housing, and it was getting cold. It was a bumpy ride, and breathing was getting to be a little uncomfortable. Hours went by, and Pengey began to think that the reason that it was so hard to breathe was because he was dead. So he decided to cooperate: he rolled over and went to sleep.

It was extremely difficult to go to sleep what with all the bumping and noise inside the wheel housing. Pengey kept busy with thoughts of his mom. He thought that he'd been a good little penguin, and soon he would see his mom in penguin heaven.

But the bumpiness kept waking him up, and now there were grinding and creaking sounds that were equally distressing.

He rolled over again, but just as he did, the wheel started to drop away from the wheel housing. Pengey could see clouds, and when he looked down he could also see land and rivers and lakes and all sorts of buildings. This was not the same as the icy land of Antarctica but a land of many structures and shapes and colors.

Pengey had no time to contemplate this new land because the wheel was descending into the air at a very rapid pace and the wind was trying to tear him off the airplane.

Pengey grabbed hold of the wheel housing. He held on with all his might. The ground was coming up at him at a ferocious speed. Within seconds the ground was upon him, and the airplane touched down.

The wheels spun and screeched and thick smoke poured off them at an astounding rate. It was yucky smoke, and it made Pengey cough and sneeze.

At last the horrifying speed began to diminish, and the plane slowed. Pengey still held on with all his might as it pulled into a space directly in front of a huge building.

When the airplane stopped, men in blue work clothes came out of the building and ran toward it. Pengey thought that the men might be after him, so he climbed as fast as he could back up into the wheel housing and hid. He stayed hidden in the wheel housing until the men finished their chores and walked back into the building.

Then, when the coast was clear, Pengey slid down the struts and onto the wheel. He looked all around—no one was watching. He needed to find a way to get inside the big albatross that had eaten Wendy.

Pengey thought that since he was still alive maybe Wendy was still alive, and it was highly probable he could still save her. Pengey jumped down onto the tarmac and looked for a way into the silver albatross.

It didn't take long to find one because there was a set of stairs that led directly up to a side entrance, and the door was open. Pengey quickly hopped up the stairs, dashed inside, and immediately became quite confused.

Inside the albatross, Pengey saw plush seats and windows and curtains and all sorts of things that humans use to make themselves comfortable. He wandered around and looked for Wendy, but she was nowhere to be seen.

Pengey sat down on one of the big cushy seats and scratched his head with his flipper. He was bewildered.

Whenever Pengey got bewildered, he pondered his options. And whenever he pondered his options, he got hungry. So he took off his little backpack, opened it, took out a piece of fish, and gobbled it up.

Just then Pengey heard voices and footsteps approaching. Panic overtook him, and he dashed toward the very darkest reaches of the airplane. He ran all the way into the tail section and hid.

After a very short while the airplane motors began to roar with life, and before very long it was speeding along again, very high in the air.

Pengey felt stuck there in the back, and to make matters worse when he reached for his backpack he found that it was gone. "Oh, no!" he thought, "I must have left it on the seat."

As Pengey pondered his options, he thought he heard Wendy's voice say, "Does something smell like fish?"

Someone who sounded like Jasper replied, "Yeah, it's not very strong, but I can smell it, too."

A moment later Wendy's voice said, "What's this?"

And the same Jasper voice said, "It's a tiny backpack."

Wendy said, "Whew, that's where the fish smell is coming from, all right."

Pengey could stand it no longer. He knew one of those voices belonged to Wendy. Still, being a very polite penguin, he wondered what the proper etiquette might be.

So he slowly crept out from his hiding place and made a rather short cooing sound. It was meant to sound like "excuse me." But he didn't know those "excuse me" words, so the cooing would just have to do.

And there he stood, Pengey Penguin, in the middle of the aisle, with his flippers sort of swaying back and forth and his right foot shyly kicking the floor.

Wendy, Jasper, and Bob were astounded to see Pengey, and they passed looks of silent amazement among themselves.

Pengey was happy to see that everyone was alive. They all smiled as Pengey bowed and cooed again. He didn't want to seem too forward, and he wondered how to approach Wendy, who appeared to be in a state of shock.

Pengey remembered that Bob and Jasper had used the word "mine" when they were talking about their fish. So Pengey tried it. He pointed to the backpack with his flipper and said, "Mine." And then he cooed and bowed to Wendy.

Hearing Pengey's voice was such a shock that Wendy fell back on her seat and passed straight out. This caused everyone great concern.

Pengey dashed to Wendy's side and fanned his little flippers around her face as fast as they would go. Everyone else gathered around wondering what to do.

Wendy came to. She opened her eyes and saw Pengey standing right there on the seat beside her.

"Pengey?" Wendy trembled.

Pengey nodded and smiled.
"

Oh, Pengey," said Wendy, "I've been so sad, I thought I'd never see you again."

Pengey cooed and patted Wendy's hand with his tiny flipper while everyone else looked on in amazement.

Wendy smiled, "You learned how to talk, didn't you."

Pengey cooed, patted her hand, and nodded yes.

Everyone smiled and breathed a collective sigh of relief. And the airplane flew on to its next stop in the city of Rio de Janeiro, in a country named Brazil.

Chapter 10

REUNITED

They had been flying along for about five hours and so, to amuse themselves, they sat close together and told stories. When it got to be Pengey's turn to tell a story, he shrugged his shoulders and hopped down to the floor.

He remained very proper, but a little of the showman came out in him. He hummed a little tune, did a little dance, and laughed and cooed all at the same time.

All the humans—Wendy, Bob, Jasper, and three new humans, George, Phyllis, and Ramon—remained completely entranced by the little penguin as they shared in his laughter or just grinned from ear to ear in amazed disbelief.

After a consummate song and penguin dance performance, Pengey hopped back onto the seat next to Wendy's amid an enthusiastic ovation. Pengey bowed a thank you to every one, and then turned his attention to Wendy, who had a frown on her face.

Wendy was still holding the tiny backpack when she looked at Pengey and asked, "Did you say, 'mine'?"

Pengey nodded his head yes, pointed at the backpack with his flipper, and said, "Mine." He pointed at Wendy with his tiny flipper and said, "Wendy." Then he laughed a most delightful laugh.

Again the humans were astounded, but it was Wendy who felt the most amazement because, after all, Pengey had said her name. She asked, "When did you learn how to talk?"

Pengey shrugged his little shoulders and kicked the seat cushion shyly.

The rest of the humans smiled and shook their heads with amazement as they resumed their conversations.

Bob said, "It's a long ways to Rio, so I'm going to take a nap." The other humans mumbled agreement and returned to their seats.

Wendy held out her hand to Pengey and said, "I'm going to keep you close to me from now on, young man."

Pengey nodded his head and walked onto Wendy's outstretched hand. She held him very softly because he was so small she thought he might break. They snuggled for a while in silence.

After a short while Pengey began to fidget, so Wendy pulled up the window shade and pointed to the view below. He climbed over her lap and tried to look out the window, but he was too short. He looked at Wendy, and she immediately got the idea and lifted Pengey so he could see out the window.

He could see the earth below with its patches of green forest and mountains, lakes, and rivers. But none of it made any sense to Pengey, because where he was born there is only ice and snow and an occasional brown rock.

Wendy put her face in the window next to Pengey's. She pointed to the scene below them and told him what he was seeing. But Pengey didn't know the words, so he just cooed and giggled and snuggled in her arms.

After a while he got bored looking out the window, so he hopped to the floor and walked to his backpack. He opened it and took out a piece of fish. But the fish had gone bad, so he dragged his backpack over to Wendy.

Wendy wrinkled up her nose and said, "These fish have gone bad, Pengey, but we can get some fresh fish as soon as we land in Rio. Is that okay with you?"

Pengey nodded in agreement and hopped back onto the seat next to Wendy.

She crinkled up her nose again at the smelly smell of Pengey's backpack. Wendy took it away from him and said, "I'll have to wash this for you, do you mind?"

Pengey shook his head no.

Wendy put some pillows next to the window and put Pengey on top of the pillows so he could see out. She said, "I'm going to wash this out. I'll be back in a minute."

He nodded and turned his attention to the textures and colors of the landscape below.

Wendy got up and went to the wash room and opened the backpack. She threw the smelly old fish away and started to wash the backpack. As she was putting it under the water faucet she saw something inside. She pulled it out and saw it was her business card.

Wendy was completely taken aback. She wondered, "How in the world did that little penguin find my business card?" She was amazed, once again, at the mind of the littlest penguin.

The card had taken on the smell of the old fish. So she threw it away and washed out the tiny backpack with hot, soapy water. She dried it with a towel and brought it out to where Pengey had been sitting.

But Pengey had snuggled on top of the pillows and under her coat and had fallen fast asleep. He was comforted by the fact that this huge thing he was flying inside of was not an albatross. But he was even more comforted by the fact that Wendy was still alive.

Wendy walked to where Jasper was seated and said, "Hey Jasper, do you still have that picture of me? The one I gave you last summer?"

Jasper looked in his wallet and took out the picture and showed it to Wendy. "You mean this one?" He laughed and said, "I had it laminated so it wouldn't wear out."

Wendy took the photograph from Jasper's hand and looked at it. It was a lovely photograph. She said, "Do you mind if I keep this for a while?"

Jasper said, "Not at all. Help yourself."

"It's for Pengey," she said.

Jasper smiled and said, "Well then, that explains it."

So Wendy took the photo, walked back to her seat, and put the picture into Pengey's backpack.

Wendy petted Pengey's head and tucked him in. It seemed to Wendy that she could see little z's coming out of

Pengey's head. She rubbed her eyes in disbelief, but when she looked again the little *z*'s were still there.

So Wendy put the clean backpack next to Pengey, lay down next to him, and fell fast asleep while the airplane flew very smoothly toward Brazil and the city of Rio de Janeiro.

Chapter 11

THE HURRICANE

Some abrupt and extremely harsh bumping interrupted Pengey's sleep. He was not alone in his sleepy confusion, as Wendy, Bob, Jasper, and all the other humans were also awakened.

The airplane was being jolted around by a vicious lightning storm. Huge bolts of electricity streaked across the sky. Pengey didn't know that he was supposed to be afraid; he thought the lightning looked pretty.

But everyone else, especially Jasper and Ramon was very upset.

Then a voice came out of the sky—actually, it was the intercom, but to Pengey it was the sky—"Ladies and Gentlemen, this is your captain speaking. We're flying along the edge of a hurricane; there is no other way around this storm. I'm very sorry for this rather rocky ride, but we should be clear of it in the next few minutes. Please take your seats and fasten your seat belts."

Pengey saw everyone immediately pull out from their seats, long ribbon-like things with big chrome buckles. They put the thick gray ribbons around their tummies and snapped them shut with the big chrome buckles.

Just then the airplane sank into an abrupt and precipitous fall, and Pengey started floating toward the ceiling. Wendy reached out and grabbed him before he bumped his head and pulled him back to the seat. But she could not strap Pengey into a seat belt because the belts were far too large for a penguin that small.

Another big bump, and Pengey went sailing off over the seat and bonked his head against the ceiling. Wendy had everything she could do to catch him and pull him back to the seat. This was a seriously bumpy ride, and Pengey was beginning to get frightened. Plus he now had a bump on his head.

Wendy held on to Pengey with one hand and untied the wide red ribbon in her hair. She tied the ribbon around Pengey, and with a great deal of effort, she tied the other end of the ribbon to the seat.

Another big bump, and Pengey remained in his seat held fast by the ribbon. Wendy and Pengey exchanged a look of relief, but the airplane ride was not getting any smoother. Over and over the bumping and the flashing of huge lightning bolts seemed to pierce the very skin of the airplane.

An hour later the rain still smashed furiously against the windows and thunder boomed in great echoing choruses all around them. The storm smashed its mighty fury into the embattled aircraft. It was a living nightmare. Everyone expected the plane to crash, but there was nothing they could do except hold on. It seemed like the plane was going to tear itself apart.

Wendy screamed, and Pengey would have jumped up to soothe her but the red ribbon held him fast in his seat. She screamed again when a bolt of lightning lit up the outside skin of the airplane. It seemed for one brief moment that the entire plane was engulfed in flames.

Pengey untied the ribbon and held on to the loose end with his flipper. He had a good grip. He leaned over to Wendy's seat and pulled the ribbon with him.

Wendy was terrified and Pengey wanted to help, so he started singing a happy little song. He made it up as he went along, but before long it started to make musical sense.

It went like this:
da, dunt, da da—da dunt da da—da dunt da
da—da dunt da da—da da, da da, da da, da
da—dunt dunt da da, da dunt da da—dunt da da
da—da dunt da da, dadadadadada . . .
and so on and so forth.

Pengey was extremely enthusiastic in his cheerful recital. And, I can assure you, even though it is rather difficult to write what a song sounds like, it was quite easy to follow if you happened to be there. Before long everyone was singing along with Pengey to his silly little tune.

After a few minutes everyone had forgotten about the storm and, just like magic, it stopped. The flying was smooth and easy, and there was barely a ripple in the air.

They sang louder.

The captain came over the intercom and thanked everyone for hanging in there with him. "This your captain speaking. I couldn't tell you before because I didn't want to cause a panic, but we were flying directly into that hurricane. We are pretty much in the clear now, but we may still experience some rough weather. It'd probably be best if you kept those seat belts on."

They all cheered.

The captain said, "And thanks to whoever made up that little song. It came just in the nick of time."

Everyone looked at Pengey and smiled.

Pengey bowed very formally and said, "I'm big."

They all cheered again, and the airplane flew off into a beautiful sunset, a little bruised and banged up but not much the worse for wear.

the bag."

Pengey cooed and tried to understand. His little eyes were melting Wendy's heart, but she knew she had to be stern with him or she'd lose him to the airport police.

The voices were at the door of the plane; there was no time to lose.

Wendy said very sternly, "Get in the bag or Wendy go bye-bye." She waved good-bye to Pengey.

Pengey started to cry and shake his head no.

Wendy softly picked him up and kissed him gently on his furry little cheek. She hushed him with a finger against his beak, winked, and placed him delicately in her travel bag. She zipped it up just as a customs officer boarded the plane.

The customs officer walked right to Wendy and said, "Is everything all right, ma'am?"

Wendy nodded pleasantly to the customs officer and said, "Why yes, everything is just fine, delightful in fact." And with that she walked off the airplane with Pengey in her travel bag, which she left unzipped just enough so Pengey could breathe.

She walked toward the terminal where there were many security guards and customs officers milling about. She approached a desk where a customs official sat.

The official smiled at Wendy and asked, "Do you have anything to declare?"

Wendy handed the customs official her passport, and, with a smile in her eyes, she said, "Not unless you want to see my pet penguin."

The customs official looked curiously at Wendy and then at his fellow officers, who all shook their heads.

The customs official looked at Wendy again and decided that she was just kidding around. "That's okay, miss. You see, both my wife and I have pet penguins." The other officers laughed while the customs official snickered and stamped Wendy's passport. He said, "You're free to go, ma'am."

Wendy said, "Thank you very much, officer." She strode through the gate, into the airport, and approached the friends who were waiting for her.

Bob, Jasper, George, Phyllis, and Ramon were all very excited as Wendy walked toward them in an unhurried and nonchalant manner. They were pointing to her and making signs that meant, "Look out!!!" and "Oh, no!!!"

Wendy noticed that other people were pointing and waving at her, too. "How very odd," she thought.

She didn't understand what the ruckus was all about until she looked down at her travel bag and saw that Pengey had popped his head out through the zippered opening. Not only was he looking around, but he was waving to all the people in the airport. The biggest problem was that the people in the airport were pointing at Pengey and waving back to him, smiling or laughing at the silly sight of the tiny penguin.

Pengey was flattered by their attention, and he laughed right along with the passersby, bowing and waving in his cheerful-but-formal penguin manner.

Wendy stopped and scolded Pengey, whispering,

"Pengey Penguin, you get back in there immediately!"

But Pengey was having way too much fun waving at all the people and making them laugh. He had no idea about the human laws and how he could get Wendy into trouble with the authorities.

Wendy decided that the only way she could remain inconspicuous, and therefore out of trouble, would be to play along with Pengey. So she started to wave at the people waving at Pengey. And, of course, they all waved back to her. It was all quite embarrassing at this point.

At last she joined up with Bob, Jasper, George, Phyllis, and Ramon and concealed her travel bag among the group. Pengey was at least out of the direct sight of the customs officers.

George looked worried, Jasper was pacing, Ramon was holding his hands over his eyes, Bob was laughing, and Phyllis was too traumatized to speak. Wendy said with a breath of relief, "Sorry, you guys. He's so polite most of the time."

Bob cut Wendy off, "There he goes!"

Wendy looked at Bob and said, "There who goes?"

Bob smiled and pointed to a large aquarium that was filled with brightly colored tropical fish. Wendy looked at Bob as if he were crazy and then looked down to her travel bag and saw that Pengey was gone. She looked back at the aquarium, where now a considerable crowd was gathered. Most of them were laughing at something. And Wendy could only conclude that it was Pengey.

"That little rascal," she said, as she dashed across the corridor to the aquarium.

The people gathered around the aquarium were all looking down at the floor. They were smiling or giggling or just plain laughing out loud.

Wendy heard one woman say, "Oh, he's just darling!"

A little girl said, "Oh Mom, he's so cute. Can we take him home?"

The crowd was getting bigger and bigger and it seemed that everyone in it was talking about taking something home.

Wendy excused her way through the crowd to where Pengey stood in the middle of the great circle of people. He was singing his little song and doing his little dance. When the people laughed and applauded, Pengey bowed and cooed.

"Oh, he's so cute," said one nicely dressed lady as she knelt down to pet him. Pengey let her pet him, and he cooed a little coo.

Wendy looked at Pengey and shouted, "Pengey! You are going to get us in a lot of trouble."

Pengey looked at Wendy, cooed, waved and bowed.

The nicely dressed lady said, "Why are you being so mean to him?"

Wendy said, "I'm sorry if it seems like I'm being mean to him. But, you see, he's just a child penguin, and he needs constant supervision. In fact, he just left Antarctica yesterday morning, and I'm afraid he's quite the little attention getter."

The nicely dressed lady said, "He doesn't seem to mind people much."

Wendy said, "Oh, no! He loves people. That's one of the problems. He's a sort of a social butterfly, you see."

A young man knelt beside them. He said, "Perhaps you should put the penguin away."

The nicely dressed lady said, "Why? For heaven sakes, he's perfectly adorable."

The young man whispered as he pointed very discreetly toward the custom's desk, "I quite agree, ma'am, but the police are coming this way, and it's probably to see what this fuss is all about."

Wendy looked up and past the throng of admiring people. She saw the police approaching. She looked back at Pengey and sternly shook her finger at him. "You're getting to be a lot of trouble, young man."

Pengey felt a little guilty, and so he kicked the floor and hung his head and cooed sadly.

Wendy quickly held out her arms to him and said, "Come on, hop up here, and I'll pretend you're a stuffed animal."

Pengey cocked his head to the side because he didn't

understand. He heard the commotion of the police asking questions. He looked at Wendy, who looked impatient, and immediately hopped into her arms. She casually stood up, turned, and walked away as if nothing had happened.

The police started to question people, but everyone was happy and so the police were confused.

Wendy joined her friends and put Pengey in her travel bag. She tried to scold him for misbehaving, but he looked so innocent. She just sighed and shook her head. She zipped her travel bag a little tighter this time.

Pengey popped his head out of the slender opening and giggled. They breathed a collective sigh of relief and walked off to find a good restaurant for lunch.

Chapter 13

THE ANCHOVY

The airport restaurant was modern and spacious. Pengey and his human entourage went in. The hostess escorted them to a table that was situated next to a very large picture window overlooking the runway.

They sat down, took their menus, and decided what to eat. Wendy heard a thrashing sound from inside her bag. Knowing it was Pengey, she unzipped the bag and out popped Pengey's head.

Pengey said, "Hi!" He was always so cheerful.

Wendy said, "You have to stay in the bag or we'll get in trouble. . . . Are you hungry?"

Pengey nodded his head and said yes.

Wendy said, "I know you don't know about restaurants, but it's where we humans often eat. I'll order some sushi, and we can share it, okay?"

"Okay."

Wendy shook her head in disbelief and mumbled, "He's actually learning how to talk. This is so strange."

She composed herself and tried to look normal. She put her travel bag next to the window so Pengey could watch the runway and the very busy goings-on of the very busy airport.

Pengey watched as airplanes took off or landed or taxied to and from various parts of the airfield. He watched all sorts of small cars and trucks and other vehicles as they scurried about, performing chores for the humans who drove them.

As the waiter approached the table, Wendy said, "Pengey, you have to hide."

Pengey said, "Okay." And Wendy placed her coat around him in such a manner that the waiter couldn't see him.

The waiter reached the table and asked for their orders. Bob, Jasper, and George ordered cheeseburgers and chocolate milk shakes; Phyllis and Ramon ordered pizza, salad, and soft drinks; and Wendy asked for two orders of sushi and a glass of white wine. The waiter walked away quite pleased with such a large order.

Pengey poked his head out from under Wendy's coat. He was very excited about something; he kept cooing and pointing his flipper at the runway. Wendy tried to see what he was all excited about, but it just looked like the normal goings-on of an airport.

He was making quite a fuss. Wendy and the others were starting to think that it might have been a bad idea to have this little penguin along. He might become more trouble than fun.

But Pengey's enthusiasm was unwavering, even though Wendy cautioned him. Before long everyone at the table was looking out the window to see what was making Pengey so excited.

Then it appeared: an immense 747 jumbo jet painted to look like a gigantic anchovy. It taxied out from behind a hanger, rolled across the runway, and took off into the sky.

Pengey fainted. It was just too much for him.

Wendy splashed some water from her glass onto Pengey's face. He started to come to. It looked to Wendy as though Pengey was smiling. She thought to herself, "He has a beak, how could he be smiling?" But when he finally sat up and rubbed his eyes with his flippers, it looked like that smile was still on his face

He trundled over to the window and looked out as the giant anchovy–painted 747 flew off into the sky. Pengey looked at Wendy, pointed at the 747 now disappearing into the clouds, and sighed deeply.

Wendy patted his little head and sighed a little, too.

Chapter 14

WASABI

At last the waiter approached with their food. The waiter served everyone and returned to the kitchen without incident.

Pengey popped out from under Wendy's coat. He was curious about what everyone had to eat.

Jasper, Bob, and George each took big bites out of their cheeseburgers, and each said, "Yum."

Ramon and Phyllis started to gobble up their pizza.

Pengey hopped up onto the table and looked at the sushi, because it sure smelled like fish.

Wendy shook a cautionary finger and said, "You're not allowed on the table." She pointed to the seat and gave Pengey a stern look. He hopped down onto the seat next to Wendy and waited for her to feed him.

Wendy cut off a piece of the sushi and held it out to Pengey, who gratefully gobbled it down. Seeing that Pengey was so hungry, Wendy continued to feed him until he slowed down a little.

She picked up a piece of fish with her chopsticks and dipped it into a little pile of green wasabi. She grinned broadly as she ate it and smiled as the rich taste of the fish and wasabi mixed in her mouth.

Wendy said, "Wow! That is some hot wasabi."

Pengey said, "Wasabi? Mine."

Wendy said, "No, Pengey. You wouldn't like wasabi. It would be too hot for you. It's people food."

She handed Pengey another piece of fish. He took it in his beak, swallowed it, and sat down with his tummy bulging.

When they had finished eating and it was getting to be time to catch the next airplane to New York City, George, Bob, Ramon, and Jasper went to the men's room to get cleaned up. Wendy and Phyllis went to the ladies' room to freshen up as well.

As Wendy got up she saw Pengey looking out the window. It was apparent that the sight of a policeman riding a horse mesmerized him. Naturally from that distance the horse looked quite small.

Pengey pointed at the horse and said, "Mine."

Wendy said, "That's a policeman. He's riding on a horse."

Pengey said, "Mine."

Wendy chuckled and said, "A horse might be a little large for you, Pengey." She could see the wonder and the ardor beaming from Pengey's eyes, so she said very softly and sincerely, "You'll probably have to get a pony."

Pengey's eyes never wavered, not so much as an iota, from the sight of that prancing horse. He said with a deep sigh, "Pony. Mine."

Wendy smiled and said, "I'll see about getting you a pony after we get to New York, but right now I want you to be good and stay here at the table, okay?"

Pengey just stared at the horse and said, "Okay."

"You watch the pony and I'll be right back."

"Pony. Mine."

Delighted with him, Wendy walked away shaking her head.

Pengey watched the horse until it pranced around to the other side of a big building. He wanted to follow it but knew he had to be good so that no one got into trouble over him.

But a couple of minutes passed, and Pengey was starting to get bored. He looked at the table and saw a piece of fish. So he hopped onto the table, picked the fish up, tucked it away, and slid his backpack over his flippers.

Then he saw the little pile of green wasabi on Wendy's plate.

Pengey said, "Wasabi. Hmmm . . . "

And without thinking another thought Pengey plunged his little beak directly into the hot wasabi. It tasted sweet at first, but within one second his whole mouth felt as if it were on fire.

If you've never heard a Penguin scream, you have missed a very loud noise.

Pengey screamed louder than any penguin had ever screamed in the whole history of penguins. He was dazed and confused. Even after he spit the fiery stuff out, his mouth, beak, and tongue felt like they were aflame.

In the hallway just outside the restaurant, Pengey could

see the aquarium with all the brightly colored fish swimming around. "Water!" he thought and made a frantic dash toward the cooling waters of the aquarium.

He wasted not a second. He dashed across the shiny floor of the airport. People seeing him coming thought that Pengey must be mad or crazy, so they got right out of his way.

He reached the aquarium and remembered how his cousin Binkey jumped so high. So Pengey jumped with all his might over the side of the aquarium and directly into the water.

There was a huge splash, water got all over the floor, and people started slipping and sliding all over the place.

Pengey washed his beak and tongue in the cool water of the aquarium.

Back in the restaurant, Bob, Jasper, and the others had just returned to the table and were looking for Pengey. But by the time Wendy approached the table they were watching the commotion at the aquarium.

Wendy had a bad feeling that Pengey was in trouble

again. And her fears were confirmed when she looked at the table and saw that Pengey was not where she'd left him.

She turned around and saw policemen and security guards surrounding the aquarium. Some of the policemen had drawn their guns and were pointing them at something she couldn't see.

Wendy ran to the aquarium and saw Pengey swimming around. He waved cheerfully to Wendy and bobbed his head over the edge as he waved happily to her again.

Everybody stared at Wendy, and she looked away, extremely embarrassed.

Pengey dove under the water and started chasing a little yellow fish around. He was having a ball for himself.

The very next moment, two men dressed in blue uniforms with the words Animal Protection Team embroidered on them approached the aquarium. One of the men was big and fat and the other was tall and skinny. The fat man carried a fishnet on a long pole, and the skinny man carried a small ladder, which he set up by the aquarium.

The fat man handed the fishnet to the skinny man, who dipped the net into the aquarium and tried to catch Pengey. But Pengey zoomed around in the water.

He was the fastest swimmer in the tank, and he was having fun chasing the little yellow fish.

That little yellow fish was Pengey's undoing, because, as Wendy watched in horror, the yellow fish swam into the net, Pengey followed it, and the skinny man in the blue uniform lifted Pengey out of the aquarium.

Pengey didn't like being wrapped up in the net. The net scared him, and he squealed the squeal of a trapped baby animal. It was a sound that Wendy had never heard before. It was a sound she never forgot.

Wendy dashed to the man with the net, but the men in the blue uniforms wasted no time in talking to Wendy or anyone else. The fat man tossed the little yellow fish back into the aquarium, and the men from Animal Protection walked away with Pengey in the net.

Pengey could see Wendy standing all by herself. She was crying and Pengey was crying, too. Pengey called out, "Wendy!"

And Wendy just stood there, quivering. She knew there was nothing she could do to save her little penguin. Crestfallen, Wendy walked back to her friends.

Little Pengey's voice called out, "Wendy! Wendy! Wendy!"

Chapter 15

THE ANIMAL POLICE

When Wendy joined her friends she was trembling and crying. She asked herself over and over how she could have been so stupid as to leave little Pengey where he could get into so much trouble. She stomped around in a tight circle and pounded her head with her fists, "Dumb, dumb, dumb."

The others tried to console her, but they also had to remind her that their airplane was ready to depart for New York in fifteen minutes. What to do? What to do? Wendy was in a quandary.

Wendy told her friends that she had to find Pengey, but she would return in time for the airplane. She had to at least try to save him. She grabbed her travel bag and ran in the direction the men in the blue uniforms had taken Pengey.

She searched and searched. She ran down one lonely corridor after another but could not find a trace of her little penguin.

As she was turning to walk back to her friends, she saw the nicely dressed lady who had admired Pengey earlier. The nicely dressed lady said, "I think I see someone who's lost a friend."

Wendy was crying too hard to speak clearly, so she just looked at the lady and nodded her head.

The lady patted Wendy on her shoulder and pointed to a small door that had no markings on it. She said, "I think if you try that door they may be able to help you."

The mere prospect of finding Pengey brightened Wendy's face. The nicely dressed lady handed Wendy a clean hanky and pointed to the door. She said, "You'd better hurry. You don't want to miss your plane." And with that the nicely dressed lady smiled at Wendy and walked away.

Wendy thanked her, dried her eyes, and walked toward the unmarked door. She knocked politely and waited for someone to answer.

The skinny man from the Animal Protection Team opened the door, smiled at Wendy, and said, "What can I do for you, Miss?"

Wendy said, "Well, you see, sir, I seem to have lost a penguin, and I was told that I might find him here."

The skinny man said, "Well, we just happen to have a penguin, but I'd have to see some sort of ownership papers before I can release him to you."

Wendy was at a loss for words. She stuttered and looked around and finally said, "Don't be silly. I don't have his papers with me, and besides, how many people have come to your office to claim a penguin today?"

The skinny man said, "I can't rightly say that there's ever been anyone at my office who's ever asked for a penguin. But, fact is, if he is your penguin, he broke the law by swimming in the aquarium, and I'm going to need to see your ownership papers."

Wendy started to cry. She cried and cried and cried. She cried so much that the skinny man started to cry, too. He said, "Now you listen here. It isn't right to make me feel this bad. I'm just doing my job."

Wendy said, "My plane leaves in just a couple of minutes. I can't leave without him."

The skinny man was crying uncontrollably, "I'm sorry, miss. I can't. They'd take my job away. Please try to understand."

"Can't I at least see him?" asked Wendy.

The skinny man was now crying even more than Wendy. He sobbed, "I know I'm going to get in trouble for this, but I just can't stand it. Follow me and I'll show you where he is. Come this way, come this way."

They walked through the small office and through another doorway into a large room filled with animal cages.

Wendy could hear Pengey's soft sobs, and she called out, "Pengey, it's me, Wendy!"

She heard Pengey's tiny voice say, "Wendy!"

The skinny man pointed, "There he is, over there."

Wendy walked to where Pengey was imprisoned in a small cage with thick iron bars. He looked very sad indeed. She said, "Silly little penguin."

Pengey said, "Silly little penguin."

Wendy laughed as tears streamed from her eyes, and Pengey cooed.

The skinny man was bewildered. "He can talk?"

Wendy smiled and said, "Just a few words, but he's a quick study."

The skinny man scratched his head and said, "Well I guess I've seen about everything now. A penguin that talks, well I'll be darned."

Just then the fat man from Animal Protection walked in with a policeman who had with him a very large dog. The policeman asked Wendy, "Is that your penguin?"

Wendy nodded and said, "Yes, I'm afraid he's caused quite a ruckus. Is that your dog?"

The policeman said, "Yes, but I'm here about the penguin. In fact the airport commissioner wants to ask you some questions. Will you please come with me?"

Wendy was terrified that something dreadful would happen to Pengey. She didn't want to leave him in that awful cage. She said, "Can Pengey come with us?"

The policeman looked a little confused and said, "Who's Pengey?"

Wendy replied in a very polite manner, "He's my Penguin. Doesn't your dog have a name?"

The policeman just looked at Wendy and said, "Wolf, his name is Wolf." Wolf barked a very loud bark.

Pengey yelled out, "Wolf!"

The skinny man said, "Wow! He sure learns fast."

Wendy said, "Yes. His mother and father were both champions."

The policeman said, "He can talk?"

Wendy nodded her head and smiled innocently.

The policeman said, "Come on, Miss, we have to get you to the commissioner's office."

"But you haven't answered my question," said Wendy.

The policeman shook his head and said, "You mean about taking the penguin with us? I'm afraid not. That is, not unless you can show us your ownership papers. You see, we have laws regarding penguins. Please come this way."

Wendy felt more panicky than ever, but she tried not to show it as she walked away from the policeman and up to Pengey's cage. She said, "I'm going to have to leave you here for a few minutes, but I want you to know that I'll be back to get you. Please don't worry, Wendy will bring you home."

Pengey said, "Wendy, home."

A voice from the intercom shouted "Wendy Fitzgerald, please report to gate twenty-five. Your airplane will depart in ten minutes."

Wendy knew she would never get Pengey back to New York City if she left him there in the animal shelter. She didn't know how to explain it to Pengey. She said to Pengey in her most soothing voice, "I'll be right back. So don't you go away."

Wendy said to the policeman, "That's my penguin, and I'm not leaving here without him."

She blew Pengey a kiss, turned quickly, and walked away with the fat man, the grumpy policeman, and his dog, Wolf.

Pengey sat in his little cage, opened his backpack, took out Wendy's card, and said, "Wendy, home."

The skinny man said, "She likes you a lot little guy."

He turned and walked away. With tears streaming down his face, he said, "I wish I had someone who liked me that much."

The skinny man turned off the lights and closed the door, and all of a sudden, except for a soft cry of loneliness from Pengey's cage, it was very quiet.

Chapter 16

LIONEL AND RUFUS

Pengey's spirits were really down in the dumps. He had to get hold of himself, but he had never seen anything like the iron bars that confined him.

He sniffed back a few more tears and pondered his options. He knew this situation was serious. And now it looked like Wendy was in trouble over him.

Pengey was determined to break out of the smelly cage that imprisoned him. He pushed against the dreadful bars with all his might, but they didn't budge. So he banged them with his little flippers and kicked them with his feet, which made a lot of noise but did not budge the bars.

A voice called out in animal talk, "Hey! Quiet down over there. I'm trying to think." Pengey looked across the narrow corridor of cages and saw a very large red, blue, and yellow macaw.

Pengey spoke animal talk quite well and responded, "Who are you?"

The macaw said, "Name's Lionel. I'm trying to escape. Who are you?"

"I'm Pengey Penguin, thank you very much."

Lionel pointed to another cage where a black-and-white bird was pecking away at his lock with his striped orange and red beak.

Lionel said, "That's Rufus; he's a puffin. He's real

smart, but he don't talk much. He's trying to escape, too."

Pengey said, "What can I do to help? Maybe we can all escape together."

Lionel said, "You might be able to help. How tall are you?"

"I'm ten inches tall, and I weigh almost four pounds."

"Can you get your flipper through the bars?"

Pengey put his backpack down, walked to the bars, and stuck his flipper in between them. "Yes, quite easily, in fact."

Lionel pointed with one of his huge wings to the top of Pengey's cage and said, "You see that long, skinny thing up there?"

"Yes."

"See if you can push it over toward Rufus's cage."

Pengey stretched for the long, skinny thing, which was the bolt that locked his cage, but he was too short to reach it. He sat down on his backpack and said, "It's no use. I'm too short."

Rufus said, "What's that thing you're sitting on?"

"It's my backpack."

"Maybe if you stand on it you can reach the lock."

Pengey didn't say anything, but he immediately got up and pushed the backpack across the floor of his cage and toward the bars. He stepped up onto the backpack and stretched as far as his flippers would go, but he was still an inch too short.

So he opened the backpack and took out Wendy's red ribbon. He stood the backpack on end and used the ribbon to tie it to the bars.

Lionel said, "What are you doing over there?"

Pengey said, "Making some adjustments."

With the backpack securely tied to the bars, Pengey hopped up on it. He stretched his flipper out toward the locking bolt and pushed on it as hard as he could. It began to move.

Pengey pushed harder and harder, and the locking bolt moved slowly out of its housing. At last it made a clicking sound as it stopped moving.

Pengey jumped down, untied the ribbon, and put it away in his backpack. He pushed on the cold steel bars and the cage door opened a crack, just enough for him to squeeze his little body out.

Pengey picked up Wendy's business card and tucked it safely into the backpack. He slipped the backpack on over his flippers, opened the cage door a little wider, and hopped down onto the floor.

"Good work, kid, said Lionel, "Now see if you can open my cage."

So Pengey set silently to work and opened Lionel's cage in very little time. Next Lionel and Pengey freed Rufus.

The three escapees let out a silent cheer of victory, but still had to escape from the room itself. It was a very large room, and the task seemed all but impossible.

Rufus said, "I'll keep a lookout." And he flew to the top of some boxes and stood next to a small window.

Pengey and Lionel huddled together to make an escape plan.

Pengey said, "I have to find Wendy. She lives in New York City."

"Hey, no problem, kid. That's where I grew up."

"Then why are you here in Brazil?"

"Because the Animal Protection League deported me."

"What does deported mean?"

Lionel said, "I was taken to New York as a baby parrot by people who were animal smugglers. They sold me to a nice man who raised me for twelve years. He was my best friend and life was good. Then the Animal Protection League found out about me, and they took me away from my master. They thought I should live in Brazil with the other Amazon parrots."

Pengey said, "That's so sad . . . it breaks my heart."

Lionel rolled his eyes and said gruffly, "It breaks my tail feathers is what it breaks. But don't worry, we'll get you home."

Rufus yelled out, "Quick, hide! Someone's coming!"

Chapter 17

THE PLAN TO ESCAPE

Pengey was in a panic. If he got caught out of his cage, it would surely make more trouble for Wendy.

But Lionel was calm and cool. He said, "Look kid, just get back in your cage. Whoever it is probably won't even check the lock. As soon as he goes, we'll make our escape."

Pengey agreed and immediately tried to hop up to his cage, but it was too high above the floor. He tried again but failed to make it.

Rufus said, "He's in the outer office. You better hurry or our goose is cooked."

Lionel said, "Here, hop on my back, I'll fly up to your cage, and then you can jump in."

Pengey tried it, but every time Lionel began to flap his wings, Pengey fell off.

"Wait," Pengey exclaimed, "I saw something on a pony one time. Maybe it will work for us." He opened his backpack and took out Wendy's red ribbon. Lionel paced back and forth while Pengey undid a tangle.

Lionel said, "This better be good, kid. Come on, hurry up."

Pengey dashed around to face Lionel and said, "Here, hold this in your beak."

Lionel opened his beak and bit down on the ribbon.

Pengey held on to the two ends of the ribbon and hopped onto Lionel's back.

Pengey said, "I'm ready. Let's go."

And with that Lionel flapped his wings, took off, and flew around the room. Pengey rode on his back holding on to Wendy's red ribbon.

Rufus yelled out, "Here he comes!"

Lionel flapped his wings mightily in front of Pengey's cage. He hung in the air like a helicopter, hovering while Pengey hopped off and into his cage.

Rufus flew down to his cage, and Lionel closed his door. Lionel walked as quickly as he could to his cage, got in, and closed his door with his powerful beak.

The office door opened, and in walked the fat man. He walked directly to Pengey's cage and looked at him.

The fat man sneered and said, "So you can talk, can you?"

Pengey looked at the fat man, bowed most politely, and said, "Yes, I'm big."

The fat man laughed out loud and said, "Well you just hold on, my little talking Penguin. I've got some people who own a circus who are very interested, and they'll pay me a lot of money for the likes of you. Yes sir, a lot of money. So don't you go away. I've got plans for you, my little feathered friend."

Pengey said, "Wendy, home."

The fat man laughed evilly, walked away, and slammed

The Plan to Escape

the door shut.

Lionel said, "Wow, man! You'd better knock off talking like a human, or you're gonna be in trouble up to your flippers."

Rufus said, "Yeah! It looks like we'd better get a move on, or you'll be working in a circus."

"What's a circus?" asked Pengey.

Rufus opened his cage door, walked out onto the floor, and said, "Come on down here, and I'll tell you all about it."

Pengey started to open his cage door when he heard the office door unlock. He hissed to Rufus, "Quick, get back in your cage." Rufus dashed back into his cage and managed to get his door closed just as the fat man walked in.

The fat man walked directly to Pengey's cage, looked at the locking bolt, and said, "Hmmm . . . I was right, it wasn't locked."

He shoved the bolt closed with a mighty bang. Then he reached in his pocket and pulled out a small brass padlock and snapped it onto the locking bolt.

* 87 *

The fat man said, "There, that ought to keep you safe and sound. But don't you worry, because those circus folks I was telling you about? They'll be here any minute. I just have to decide first which one I'm going to sell you to."

The fat man laughed maniacally as he walked away and slammed the door shut.

Pengey was frightened. All he could say was "Wendy, home."

Lionel popped out of his cage and so did Rufus. They were both extremely upset after overhearing the fat man's plans to sell Pengey to the circus. They flew up to Pengey's cage and landed on it.

Lionel said, "It's one of those locks that has a key. My master used to have one. We'll never get it open unless we can get the key."

Rufus said, "I have no idea how to get that thing open, but the fact is, they are going to sell Pengey to the circus, come sunshine or high water. So if we can't break him out of here, we'll have to break him out of the circus."

Pengey said, "I don't know what you two are dreaming up, but if it gets me out of this cage, I'll be a happy penguin."

"It's a long shot, kid," said Lionel "But it's the only shot we've got."

"What's a long shot?"

Rufus said, "A chance, Pengey . . . a slim chance."

Lionel said, "Just play it cool, kid, real cool, get me?"

Pengey said, "I'll try. I should be good at playing it cool 'cause I'm from Antarctica."

Rufus and Lionel nodded to each other and flew back to the floor and made a huddle. Pengey sat on his backpack and awaited his fate. He could hear a ruckus on the floor around all the other cages, but he didn't care because a moment later he heard Wendy's voice. She was outside the office in the corridor and she was yelling for Pengey, but the fat man would not let her in.

Pengey sat very still, and a tear rolled down across his tiny beak.

Chapter 18

THE MAD SCIENTIST

Meanwhile out in the hallway, the fat man and the policeman with his dog, Wolf, were taking Wendy to her airplane.

Wendy shouted, "I'm not leaving until I have Pengey!"

The fat man said, "If you do not get on that airplane then you will have to go to jail."

The policeman pushed Wendy along and said, "Right this way, ma'am."

Wendy was crying, but she didn't know what to do because she certainly didn't want to go to jail. She cried out in vain, "HELP! Somebody help! Please help me!" But everyone in the airport looked away because they were afraid of the policeman and his terrible dog.

Wendy yelled, "YOU MONSTER! You let Pengey go!"

She called out to Pengey, hoping he could hear her, "Pengey, Pengey! I'll come back for you, I promise!"

And so the policeman hurried Wendy down the long, abandoned corridors toward the departure gate and the airplane.

She complained that this was cruel and unusual punishment for such a small penguin. "After all," she said, "he's really very small, and he didn't mean to go swimming in the aquarium. And, having just arrived from Antarctica, how would he know about the law forbidding swimming in the aquarium in the first place?"

Her speech fell on the policeman's deaf ears. He just nodded and kept Wendy moving on toward her departure gate and her airplane.

The fat man rubbed his greedy hands together and watched the policeman roughly escort Wendy away. He turned to see three men approaching him. They were arguing bitterly among themselves but calmed down as they got closer to the fat man.

One, the ringmaster, was short and stocky. He wore a top hat and a red coat and long, shiny black boots. He had a long, black, droopy mustache and his face wore a sinister look.

Another, the animal trainer, was tall and muscular. He carried a whip and wore a khaki-colored uniform and brown lace-up boots. He looked mean.

The last, the mad scientist, was a pear-shaped man with a big belly and skinny little shoulders. He wore a white lab coat and thick, round glasses. The more you studied him, the more you felt that there was something undeniably evil about him.

The fat man looked happy as the others approached. He bowed to them and said, "Did you bring the money?"

The mad scientist said with a heavy German accent, "Vee vill see about ze money ven vee see zis talking penguin. Vat was ze name of his master?"

The fat man grinned evilly and said, "Her name was Wendy Fitzgerald."

He pointed to the office door and said, "And she is no longer of any consequence, but her prize is right this way, gentlemen.

. . . But I'm afraid I'm going to have to see the color of your money before any of you see the penguin."

The ringmaster said, "I have no problem showing you my money, but wouldn't it be wiser to step into someplace more private?"

So the fat man smiled confidently, opened the door to the outer office, and they all went in.

Meanwhile back in the cage room, Lionel and Rufus had freed all the other animals.

There were two garden snakes, Ralph and Betty. There were two cats, Miffey and Tabby. There were two pigeons, Coo and Burp. There were seven field mice, Edna, Pete, Serg, Terrance, Rhonda, Pepe, and Aaron. There were two small dogs, Spot and Jake. And there were two monkeys, Chip and Alexia. Lionel was giving them all their final instructions when he heard the outer door open and close.

Lionel said, "Okay, listen up. We might not all make it out in this break, but we're going to give it our best shot. Now go and hide, and when these guys from the circus come in to get Pengey we make a run for the door and try to trip 'em up. That'll scare them enough to drop Pengey, and he can escape on my back when I fly away—sound good?"

They all mumbled assurances and nodded in agreement, scattered into the dark corners of the room, and took their hiding places.

Rufus called out, "Don't do anything before Pengey is out of his cage."

Lionel said, "Hey kid, remember they only want you because you can talk people talk. So whatever you do, do—

not—talk—Human."

"Okay, my beak is sealed," said Pengey. And he sat down on his backpack.

Lionel and Rufus went back into their cages and closed their doors. The door from the office opened and in walked the mad scientist, the fat man, the animal trainer, and the ringmaster.

The fat man pointed to Pengey's cage and said, "There he is gentlemen, the next wonder of the world—a talking penguin."

The ringmaster walked up to Pengey's cage, looked at him, and said in a disappointed tone of voice, "He's kind of small for an emperor penguin." Pengey stuck his tongue out at the ringmaster, made a loud raspberry noise with his beak, and returned to staring gloomily at the wall of his cage.

The ringmaster was very insulted and said in shock, "Why, did you see that? He stuck his tongue out at me." Lionel wanted to laugh, but he held it in and silently congratulated Pengey for his nerve.

The animal trainer stepped up to Pengey's cage and looked at Pengey in a very mean way. But Pengey was too depressed to notice him. He just turned his back to the animal trainer, who said, "Why that obstinate little Penguin, he just turned his back to me." Then he added in a threatening voice, "He'll not be so obstinate after he feels the sting of my whip."

The mad scientist approached and looked quietly at Pengey. He didn't say anything. Then he said, "Vell, vell, vell . . . look vat vee have here. A fine example of ze emperor penguin . . . yes, yes, yes . . . a fine example indeed."

The mad scientist turned to the fat man and said, "He certainly is a handsome specimen. I must zay, von of zee most perfect I have ever zeen."

The fat man felt quite proud of having caught Pengey because of the mad scientist's compliments. He puffed up his chest proudly and said, "Yes, to be sure. I knew I had quite a catch when I found him."

The mad scientist was a very crafty fellow, and he lured Pengey into his trap when he said, "But zis fine specimen is not zer penguin zat talks, is it?"

The fat man was confused by the mad scientist, but he answered, "But it is. It is the penguin that I told you about. Hey you, say something," he commanded Pengey.

Pengey ignored the fat man.

The fat man shouted, "I told you to talk! Now say something!"

Pengey turned and stuck his tongue out at the fat man, who was very insulted and said, "You can't stick your tongue out at me."

Pengey blew a raspberry at the fat man, who looked like he was now going to explode.

The mad scientist said, "Please, enough of zis shouting."

His calm manner fooled Pengey. Pengey's eyes began to wander in the direction of the scientist, who rubbed his chin, and said, "He is too perfect to be zer penguin zat speaks. He looks hungry, have you fed him?"

"No."

The mad scientist turned to Pengey and said, "There, there, you mustn't look so sad. Vood you like zomething to eat? Wendy told me to give zis delicious fish to you." And at that the mad scientist held out a fresh anchovy to Pengey.

But Pengey wouldn't look at the mad scientist. He shifted uncomfortably on his backpack, sighed deeply, and said sadly, "Wendy, home."

The mad scientist looked at the fat man and said, "Remarkable. Absolutely astonishing." He spoke to Pengey very softly, "Yes, Wendy home. Wendy said to give you zis nice fish."

The mad scientist looked harshly at the fat man and shouted, "Open zis terrible cage, you are distressing zis penguin. You are making zis penguin depressed."

"Yes, sir," said the fat man, and he opened Pengey's cage immediately.

The mad scientist dangled the anchovy in front of Pengey and then drew it away. Pengey's head followed the fish, so that now Pengey was facing him.

The mad scientist said, "I have more of zeeze anchovies. Wendy said you vud like some."

Pengey nodded his head yes, but he didn't speak.

The mad scientist said, "I thought you vud be more well mannered zan zis. After all, you emperor penguins are supposed to be very polite."

Pengey didn't want anyone to think he wasn't polite, so he stood up and bowed to the mad scientist. He said, "Fish. Yum."

The mad scientist shook his head in disbelief and simply said, "Remarkable."

He held an anchovy to Pengey's beak, Pengey sniffed it, then took a bite. He spit it out immediately, because it didn't taste right. In very the next moment he felt very sleepy, and a moment later he swooned onto the cage floor, fast asleep.

The mad scientist said, "There, he von't be giving us any trouble now." As he walked away, he said to the animal trainer, "Take him with us, and treat him gently. He is worth more zan all the gold and diamonds in ze world."

The mad scientist turned to the fat man, handed him an envelope, and said, "Here is your twenty-five thousand dollars. He vill make excellent research material indeed. I vill clone him many times. Vee must be going."

They turned to leave, and just as the fat man opened the door, Lionel yelled, "Charge!" All the little animals sprang out from their hiding places and attacked the evil humans.

The two snakes, Ralph and Betty, crawled out from behind a box next to the door and bit the fat man in the ankle. The fat man screamed in pain, fell down and bonked his head, and passed out. Ralph and Betty quickly slipped away to the safety of the garden.

The two cats, Miffey and Tabby, jumped upon the ringmaster and scratched him, but his boots were too thick for their claws to hurt him and he tossed them off. They ran for their lives and escaped unharmed.

The two pigeons, Coo and Burp, flew around the mad scientist making it difficult for him to see. But he brushed them off, and they flew off to save their lives.

The seven field mice, Edna, Pete, Serg, Terrance, Rhonda, Pepe, and Aaron, surrounded the animal trainer and tried to trip him up. But ultimately they had to get out of the way of his heavy boots. Miraculously, they all got away without any injury.

The two small dogs, Spot and Jake, ran up and bit the animal trainer on his ankles and then ran away, out into the corridor and on to freedom.

The two monkeys, Chip and Alexia, grabbed the animal trainer's whip and escaped with it as he fell to the floor, holding his ankle in pain.

But the animal trainer still held on to Pengey. The ringmaster wasn't hurt, and the mad scientist was more determined than ever to take Pengey to his research laboratory.

With Pengey as their captive the hateful three made a quick dash for their car, which was waiting just outside the office-building door.

Lionel flew up to Pengey's cage, grabbed his backpack in his beak, and flew down to meet Rufus. He put the backpack down and said, "Poor kid. He's gonna need some help, and for some reason, he's gonna need this, too. We'd better take it with us."

Rufus nodded in silent agreement. Lionel grabbed the backpack in his beak. He and Rufus quickly walked into the corridor and followed the demented three and the captive Pengey.

They flew onto the rooftop of the mad scientist's car as it drove away toward an ill-omened castle on the outskirts of the city.

Dark clouds began to loom overhead, and lightning bolts could be seen striking the dark castle in the distance. The car raced on.

Chapter 19

CAPTURED

The mad scientist's car zoomed away from the airport. Pengey was unconscious and helpless and still at the mercy of the demented animal trainer. They were going very fast, careening around corners with tires screeching.

Rufus fell off and had to fly to keep up. Lionel thought that whoever was driving must be crazy, and so he jumped off and flew alongside of Rufus. They stayed a comfortable distance from the car, flying along at about forty feet in the air.

Meanwhile, inside the car, the ringmaster, the mad scientist, and the animal trainer were still arguing.

The ringmaster said, "I don't see why you should have him first. We have all put up money. I want him in my circus tonight."

The animal trainer said, "He should be mine first. He needs to feel the sting of my whip so he learns to behave."

The mad scientist yelled, "Silence! You shall all have your turn with him. But what is important is zat he is properly cloned, so ve can sell copies of him."

Lionel and Rufus watched as the car traveled at frightful speed, lurching and skidding its way onto a narrow country road.

Up the mountain road went the car, screeching its way around tight corners and past the edges of jagged cliffs with precipitous drops. Up and up the craggy mountain they raced until they screeched to a stop at the entrance of the mad scientist's evil castle.

Pengey was awake and making such a fuss it was difficult for the animal trainer to hold on to him.

Rufus and Lionel flew up and landed on the castle's roof, where they watched Pengey's struggle from on high.

Rufus balled up his wing into a fist and said, "Why, I oughtta fly down there and let 'em have it."

Lionel said, "Chill out, chum. We're going to have to wait for the right time. There ain't no sense in either one of us gettin' hurt or captured."

"I guess you're right," said Rufus. "But still, I'd like to teach those guys a thing or two."

Lionel said, "Patience, dude. Our turn will come."

Down in the courtyard, Pengey, who had just regained consciousness, was putting up a valiant struggle, especially when you consider that he only weighed four pounds and was a mere ten inches tall. He flapped his little flippers and kicked with his little feet. Then he bit the animal trainer on the finger.

The animal trainer screamed in pain but managed to hold on to Pengey.

Pengey yelled out, " Let me go!"

But the animal trainer was big and strong, and he held on to Pengey with all his might. In the next few moments, Pengey was pulled into the castle.

Lionel and Rufus could do nothing but look on at Pengey's impending doom.

Chapter 20

THE EVIL EXPERIMENT

The animal trainer had everything he could do to hold on to Pengey, who bit him again in the same spot, kicked his feet, squirmed with his little body, and flailed with his flippers.

The mad scientist walked directly into his laboratory and over to some very large and strange-looking machines with large dials and buttons and many lights of different colors. He turned on all of the machines, and they began to hum menacingly.

The mad scientist told the animal trainer and the ringmaster to tie Pengey down to an operating table located in the center of the laboratory. The animal trainer used four small leather straps to tie Pengey to the table.

Pengey struggled against the leather straps and tried to kick the animal trainer. But it was no use because he was not strong enough to break the thick straps. So he bit the animal trainer again on the same spot, and again the hateful animal trainer yelped in pain.

The ringmaster stood by with a gleeful, wicked look on his face and rubbed his hands together in a sinister fashion. He said to the mad scientist, "When will you be done with him? I want him for tonight's circus show."

The mad scientist replied harshly, "Do not rush me. Procedures as complex as these must be done delicately."

He pointed to some tubes that were connected to the menacing machines and said to the ringmaster, "Bring those tubes to ze operating table. Quickly! There is no time to lose."

The mad scientist approached the operating table carrying with him a large hypodermic needle and commanded, "Hold him still. Vee are making ze final preparations for ze cloning."

The animal trainer had all he could do to keep little Pengey down, even with the leather straps. Pengey struggled and kicked and struggled some more. He kept thinking of Wendy and how he had to get back to her. He kept trying to bite the animal trainer.

The ringmaster approached the operating table holding the long tubes from the foul machines in his hands.

The machines buzzed and clicked and hummed. Their lights blinked and flickered, and their dials twisted and spun in a frenzied fashion, as if they were totally out of control.

The mad scientist said, "Good, now put ze tube with ze funnel over the penguin's beak. He vill be unconscious in a matter of moments."

The ringmaster did as he was told. And, as much as Pengey struggled, the ether that poured out of the tube and through the funnel put him into a deep sleep.

Instantly he was caught in a whirlwind of dark and cryptic dreams. His mind raced into the deepest reaches of sleep, and at last he struggled no more.

The mad scientist shouted at the ringmaster, "Do not give him too much! He must be semi-conscious for ze experiment to succeed." Then, seeing Pengey's deep sleep, he yelled at the ringmaster, "You bloated idiot! You've ruined ze attempt. Vee vill have to wait for ze anesthetic to wear off."

He gave the ringmaster a hard look and said, "If zhere

is any damage to the penguin, I vill hold you personally responsible. AM I MAKING MYSELF PERFECTLY CLEAR?"

The ringmaster backed away from the operating table, and the animal trainer stood back, too. They were terribly afraid of the mad scientist because his power was so great.

Just then one of the big machines began to blink all of its lights. The humming sound had instantly become very loud, and all the dials spun uncontrollably. Suddenly smoke began to pour out of the machine.

"Quickly!" The mad scientist shouted, "Shut it off!"

The ringmaster raced to the machine and shut off all the switches, but the smoke continued to pour out and fill the room.

"Fools, ze machine is on fire!" the mad scientist shouted again. "Open all the windows!" The ringmaster and the animal trainer raced to the windows and opened them wide.

Meanwhile from up on the rooftop, Lionel and Rufus could see the smoke billowing out of the laboratory windows and into the courtyard.

Lionel said, "Oh, no! Look!"

Rufus said, "This doesn't look too good for our little friend."

Lionel said, "We're going to have to get in through one of those open windows, and we're going to have to do it fast. With that much smoke, Pengey's not going to last very long."

Rufus said, "I can hold my breath longer than you. I'll get in as fast as I can. I'll find him. If he's in there, I'll find him."

With that Lionel and Rufus flew down to the courtyard. They landed on the branch of a tree next to an open window where the smoke was not so thick.

"Hold your breath and keep your eyes open," said Lionel. "Go quickly, there's not a moment to lose."

Rufus took a huge breath, flapped his wings as hard as he could, and zoomed in through the open window.

At the same time, the ringmaster, the animal trainer, and the mad scientist all raced out of the laboratory, leaving Pengey to breathe the acrid smoke and fumes.

Rufus flew around the room, but it was hard to see anything from up near the ceiling. Still holding his breath, he dove down and straightened out just before crashing into the floor. Now almost out of breath, he zoomed around at low level and saw Pengey lying on the operating table. He had to breathe, and so he flew out to where Lionel was anxiously waiting.

Lionel said, "Well?"

Rufus huffed and puffed, "He's in there all right. They've got him strapped to some sort of table. The smoke is almost on top of him. We've got to move fast." Rufus coughed from the smoke, and Lionel patted his back. "You gonna be okay?"

"I'll be fine, but if we don't get Pengey out of there pretty soon he might not make it."

"Where is he?"

"In the middle of the room, but you can't do it by yourself. It'll take the both of us to untie him from the table and then tie him to you."

Lionel said, "Lead the way, my friend."

Rufus said, "Follow me and hold your breath."

So in went Lionel and Rufus. They flew through the dense smoke and landed on the operating table. They immediately began to release Pengey from his leather straps.

Lionel got frustrated, so he bit through the straps with his powerful beak and tossed them on the table. He put his ear to Pengey's chest. "He's barely breathing. We have to get him out of here in a hurry."

Rufus coughed, "This side's untied. Toss me the backpack."

Lionel tossed Pengey's backpack to Rufus, who caught it before it fell off the table.

Lionel said, "You'll have lift him onto my back, then tie him to me with the red ribbon."

Rufus busied himself with lifting Pengey, and Lionel squatted down as low as he could go.

Just then Pengey started to come to.

Lionel said, "He's comin' around."

Rufus said, " Pengey, can you hear me?"

Pengey could see the faint outline of Rufus, but he was still under the spell of the powerful anesthetic. He said with a very sleepy voice, "Yes, I can hear you." Then he fell fast asleep again.

Rufus shook him and shook him. One of Pengey's eyes

opened, and he said, "Rufus! How did you get here?"

He started to swoon away again, but Lionel shook him and said, "You've got to stay awake, kid."

The whole room was filled with smoke, and the big machine now burst into flames.

"Let's go my friend," said Lionel. " This whole place could blow up any second."

Rufus pushed Pengey onto Lionel's back and said, "Come on, Pengey. There you go. Now hold on."

Pengey groaned and fastened his beak onto Lionel's neck feathers. Rufus wrapped Wendy's red ribbon around Pengey and then around Lionel's neck. Then he took the leather straps and tied them around Pengey's waist and onto Lionel's chest.

Rufus gave Lionel the two ends of the ribbon and said, "Hold on to these with your beak, and pump as hard as you can—he's heavier than he looks."

Lionel started to beat his wings just as the mad scientist, the ringmaster and the animal trainer rushed back into the room, each carrying a fire extinguisher. Lionel flapped as hard as he could as he ran toward the edge of the operating table with Rufus pushing on his tail feathers for extra momentum.

Rufus gave one last shove, then spread his own wings to take off smoothly into the smoke-filled room.

Lionel spread his wings and fell precipitously toward the floor. But he pumped and he pumped and flapped as hard as he could, and, just as he was about to hit the floor, his wings lifted him, and off he went with Pengey strapped to his back.

Pengey had passed out again. He stayed on Lionel's back only because Rufus had done such a good job of tying him on with the leather straps.

In the next moment, Lionel, Rufus, and the unconscious Pengey emerged from the chamber of smoke and fire. They flew up to the rooftop, where they knew they wouldn't be spotted.

Down below, the entire laboratory was engulfed in flames, and the mad scientist, the animal trainer, and the ringmaster were running out of the castle yelling and screaming for help.

Chapter 21

FREE AT LAST

While the evil castle and laboratory were consumed by flames and the mad scientist, the ringmaster, and the animal trainer ran for their lives, Lionel and Rufus laid Pengey onto the safety of the roof.

Pengey moaned and groaned, "Wow, . . . what a headache."

Lionel said, "Look, kid, we're not out of the woods yet."

Pengey looked around and said, "I don't see any woods."

Rufus rolled his eyes and said, "What Lionel's trying to say is, we're not out of danger yet."

Pengey looked over the edge of the roof and was immediately in a state of shock. "How did I get up here?" he gulped.

"Lionel. He flew up here with you on his back."

"How are we going to get down?"
"
The same way I got up here, kid. How you feelin'?"

Pengey tried to stand up but was very wobbly. He sat back down and held his head. Then he looked at Lionel and said, "I'm not up to snuff, but I'm willing to try anything if it gets me away from here and back to Wendy."

Lionel said, "That's the spirit."

Rufus put Pengey's backpack down beside him and said, "Come on, we've got a long ways to go."

Pengey stood up, slid his backpack over his flippers, and tied Wendy's red ribbon around Lionel's beak. He tied the leather straps around Lionel's chest and gave them a good yank.

The leather straps felt secure, and so Pengey walked around and climbed up onto Lionel's back. He felt wobbly as he tucked his feet into the leather straps, but there he sat, ready for takeoff.

It was almost sunset, the time that most birds go to sleep. But the brave threesome decided it would be best to get as far away from the evil castle as they could before nightfall.

Lionel spread his wings and headed due north, the direction of New York City, with Rufus by his side and little Pengey riding on his back. When they had flown about a mile, the evil castle exploded into a million billion pieces.

They flew off toward the protection of the high trees deep in the forest.

Pengey was more or less jolted awake now, not only from the noise of the explosion, but because he was flying along on Lionel's back at around forty miles per hour. He was a little unsteady at first, but he quickly got the hang of it. The fresh air did all of them good.

Holding on to that red ribbon was more like holding on to the reins of a horse than just a plain ribbon. The leather straps kept Pengey snug against Lionel's back. He felt safe and secure even though he was flying a hundred feet in the air.

About twenty miles from the castle, Lionel began to look for a place to touch down for the night. It was starting to get too dark to fly. Just then he spotted a huge Brazil nut tree. He called to Rufus, "Over there, we'll be safe for the night."

Rufus nodded and called back, "It's okay with me, but what are we going to eat? I'm starving."

It was too late. Lionel was at the Brazil nut tree, landing on an extremely thick branch near the top.

Pengey was too scared to get off, but Lionel kept walking around and that was even bumpier than flying. So Pengey jumped off and stammered, "W-would you please tell me what we are doing so high up in this tree?"

Rufus laughed, while Lionel rolled his eyes, and said, "Look, kid, the ground down there is crawling with all sorts of animals—animals that wouldn't think twice about making a dinner out of you, or me or Rufus, for that matter. Think of it as a safety thing."

Pengey said, "I never thought of that."

Rufus said, "Look, you guys, I saw a fish stand about three miles back. It's probably closed for the night, but there might be some scraps lying around. I'll try to bring something back for you, Pengey."

"Thank you, Rufus. I mean, I appreciate it very much." Pengey bowed his most formal bow, and Rufus took wing and was gone.

Lionel paraded around and gathered leaves and small branches and placed them in the crotch of the very large branch of the very large tree. In a few minutes he had built up a sizable cushion of material.

Pengey asked very politely, "May I ask what you're doing?"

"Makin' a nest for you to sleep in."

Pengey said, "A nest? But I've never slept in a nest before."

Lionel said, as he packed more leaves into the nest," Correct me if I'm wrong, but ain't you a bird?"

Pengey said, "Well, I am a bird. But we emperor penguins, while we adhere to all sorts of bird mannerisms, don't make nests. We sleep on the ice or the ground but not in trees."

Lionel said, "Well, you're gonna sleep in this nest tonight."

"But I don't know how to sleep in a nest."

Lionel said, "You don't know how to fly either, kid. So do me a favor, sleep in the nest. I don't want to wake up in the morning and see you in pieces at the bottom of the tree."

Pengey started to stutter a protest, "I . . . I . . . B-but . . "

Lionel cut him off and said, "It's easy, kid. Just put your flipper up over your eye, and go to sleep."

About a minute later Rufus flew back into the tree. He was out of breath, acting very strangely, and some of his feathers seemed to be missing or ruffled. Pengey noticed the damage and was shocked.

Rufus dropped six little fish from his beak onto Pengey's nest and said, "These are good. Save a couple for me."

Lionel said, "What happened?"

"Remember the animals we were talking about? Well, I forgot that cats like fish, too. They were all over me as soon as I landed. I was lucky to get away with this."

Pengey asked in his most considerate voice, "Are you hurt?"

Rufus said, "One of them did scratch me, but I don't think there's any real harm done."

Lionel said, "Yeah? You can't be too careful with a cat scratch. In the morning, we'd better fly to the ocean and wash your wound in saltwater."

Rufus nodded agreement, and Pengey looked at the fish. It was a fish he'd never seen before, but since puffins are experts on fish, Pengey took his word that they would taste good. They sat down on the nest that Lionel had built and started to eat a very meager meal.

Lionel said, "You sure those cats didn't see where you landed?"

Rufus said, "It's a long way off for a cat. Besides it's almost dark, so how could they follow me?"

"That's a cinch. You're a black bird with a white chest, pretty easy to spot at sunset."

"It's a chance we'll have to take."

Lionel said, "I'll think about that after I find something to eat. There's got to be some ripe nuts on this tree." And he walked off through the maze of branches.

Pengey ate one of the fish, and it tasted good. Rufus gobbled down another. Pengey asked, as he chewed away on his second fish, "How did you manage to get to Brazil?"

Rufus said, "It was a total calamity. The animal relocations team was suppose to send my wife and I to the state of Maine, somewhere along the coast where they are trying to bring back the puffins who used to live there. I got put on the wrong boat and ended up in Rio. I've been here for almost three months." He picked up another fish, swallowed it whole, and sighed, "I'd just like to get back to my wife and our baby puffin. I'm sure she's almost grown by now."

Lionel walked back to the nest and sat down, his beak filled with Brazil nuts. He tossed them onto the nest and said, "At least there's lot's to eat." Then he frowned and said, "I think we should take turns sleeping. Whoever's up watches for the cats and anything else that moves. Agreed?"

Pengey nodded and Rufus said, "I'll take the first watch."

And so our valiant band of heroes camped in the highest branches of the Brazil nut tree. They finished their skimpy meals, and one-by-one they fell asleep.

Rufus took the first watch. He looked across the vast expanse of the now-darkened forest to the hazy and distant outline of the Atlantic Ocean. But he watched the forest below closely; he watched for anything that moved because, after all, cats are exceedingly quiet and extremely good hunters.

The scratch on Rufus's wing was beginning to hurt. He didn't want to complain. He hoped he would be able to fly in the morning.

Lionel took the second watch. Hour after hour they kept

their vigil, and the night passed without any sign of the cats.

Pengey, completely exhausted from his ordeal, slept the night away with his head tucked underneath his little flipper. As unfamiliar as it was, he was able to sleep in the nest after all.

Chapter 22

CAT SCRATCH FEVER

It was a very long night, indeed. When daybreak arrived, neither Lionel nor Rufus felt very rested. Pengey was up at the crack of dawn because of his concern over the cat scratch on Rufus's wing. It certainly was among the reasons that jolted Rufus from his sleep all night. It had obviously become painful and inflamed. It looked like he had a deep infection setting in.

Still Rufus said nothing; he complained not a peep. And so with a little preparation, Pengey climbed onto Lionel's back and grabbed hold of Wendy's red ribbon.

Rufus flapped his wings; the pain was bad, but he was willing to try to make a dash for the shoreline of the Atlantic some twenty miles away.

Pengey said, "We go on three. One. Two. THREE!"

Rufus took off and flew rather slowly, but they had a good tailwind and it made for fairly easy going. Lionel flew alongside Rufus in case anything went wrong.

Pengey held on to the reins of red ribbon and enjoyed the ride but remained deeply concerned about Rufus and his injured wing.

They flew over the outskirts of Rio and above the vast countryside. They flew over farms and small forests.
The sun felt hot, and yet it was only six o'clock in the morning.

It didn't take long for them to reach the Atlantic. The cliffs at land's end plummeted sharply into the warm ocean waters. There were many small, sandy beaches, which would have been hard to find unless you just happened to be a bird.

They landed on one such tiny beach and rested. Rufus immediately dove into the salty water. The salt made his cat scratch sting and throb. He knew he was getting sick but didn't know what to do about it. He looked down into the water and saw many little fish swimming around eating krill. But his wound was too tender for him to dive after them.

Rufus walked up onto the beach and plopped down on the sand. His normally bright, orange-red beak had practically turned gray.

Pengey said, "Gee, Rufus, you look terrible."

Lionel said, "I'll second that."

Rufus didn't say anything; he just curled up on the sand and held his injured wing.

Pengey asked, "Are you hungry?"

Rufus nodded and held on to his wing. He was in great pain. Lionel paced back and forth.

Pengey looked worried, and when Pengey got worried he pondered his options.

He had a lot of his waterproof feathers now, and so he walked to the water's edge. He looked very much the mature penguin, only he was very short.

Lionel said, "Where do you think you're going, kid?"

Pengey said, "Fishing."

And without another word, he dove headlong into the

ocean. He dove very deep—almost one hundred meters. He was surprised that he could see so well and that it was easy to hold his breath. He swam around at frightening speeds and gobbled up lots and lots of krill.

Next he saw a small squid swim by. It swam really fast but not nearly as fast as Pengey. And so Pengey hunted it down and gobbled it up. He saw a school of little fish like the ones that Rufus found the night before. So he chased them down, caught three, and held them in his beak while he made the swim back to the surface.

Lionel and Rufus were both pacing back and forth and calling Pengey's name. They both looked extremely worried.

Pengey popped out of the water and onto the sandy beach, but he couldn't talk because he had all those little fish in his mouth.

Lionel ran to Pengey's side and said, "Boy, am I glad to see you. We thought you were dead. No one can stay underwater that long."

Pengey walked to where Rufus was sitting and dropped the fish. "Here, eat these, they'll help you get better," he said.

Rufus asked, "But how could you stay under the water for so long?"

Pengey shrugged and said, "I don't know, but it was easy."

Lionel said nervously, "B-but, you must have been underwater for more than five minutes."

Pengey shrugged again and walked back to the water and dove in. He swam around for a while and popped back onto the shore.

"There's so many fish. Do you want some more?"

Rufus said, "I'm still hungry, if you don't mind."

Lionel walked up to Pengey and said, "Look, kid, I haven't eaten since last night, so I'm going to fly back to the Brazil nut tree and find breakfast. You take care of Rufus, okay?"

Pengey nodded and asked, "Is there anything special I should do?"

"Just make sure he keeps soaking his wing in the ocean water. The salt is good for his wound. I'll be back in an hour." And with that Lionel lifted off with a short run and the flapping of his mighty wings.

Pengey helped Rufus to his feet, and they walked down to the water's edge. He said, "Sit here in the shallow water and keep soaking your wing."

"Where are you going?"

"To get some dessert. Want some?"

Rufus found it difficult, but he smiled and nodded. He was in severe pain. He held his wing because the infection was getting really bad. He started to doze off. Pengey knew he had to keep Rufus awake so he could keep bathing the infection in the salty ocean water.

Pengey shook him and said, "Rufus, wake up!"

Rufus groaned, "Sorry, I guess I was falling asleep."

"You have to keep bathing your wing or the infection will set in."

Rufus said, "I feel sort of sick all of a sudden."

Pengey said, "You have to keep your mind off it. Why don't you tell me a little about yourself."

"There's not really much to tell."

"There's always something to tell. For instance, how did your parents come to name you Rufus?"

Rufus laughed and said, "It's kind of funny. But when I was a baby, my beak was bright red. My folks thought I should have a name that went along with my beak. So they came up with Rufus."

"You wouldn't know it to look at it now. It looks kind of gray."

Rufus chuckled and said, "Yeah, it turns gray when I have a cold, too."

Pengey and Rufus whiled away some more time chatting about the old days until Pengey asked, "Think you can stay awake now?"

"Yeah, I feel a little better."

"Good. How about that dessert?"

"Sounds great, Pengey."

Pengey dove into the water and went hunting for more small fish. They were easy to catch, and so within a few minutes Pengey popped back onto the shore and dropped the fish at Rufus's feet.

Rufus chose a fish, gobbled it up, and said, "Mmm! These are really good. Thanks, Pengey."

Pengey walked back to the water and dove in. He yelled out to Rufus, "It's too hot for me on the beach, so I'll be swimming around. After you finish eating dessert, you have to come back in and soak your wing."

Rufus sat at the water's edge soaking his infected wing and nodded agreement.

And so Pengey, Lionel, and Rufus spent three days on that beach. Pengey kept cool by fishing all day. He stuffed himself on krill and little squids. He hunted for Rufus and brought him a wide variety of little fish. Pengey also practiced deep diving and holding his breath.

Rufus and Lionel worried when he did that, especially Rufus, because puffins can only hold their breath for less than a minute. But Pengey could stay underwater for over fifteen minutes. And when he popped out of the water, he was the same happy, bouncy little penguin he'd always been—no worse for wear.

This confused Rufus, but he was grateful to Pengey for feeding him, especially while he was sick. Without Pengey, Rufus surely would have died and gone to puffin heaven.

Rufus kept soaking his wound in the salt water, and before the end of the third day, his wound was completely healed and he felt as good as new.

The day was quickly coming when they would be leaving the safety of that little beach. It was time to go to New York City.

It was time for Rufus to go on to Maine and find his baby and his wife, for Lionel to find his old master, and for Pengey to find Wendy.

Rufus rested in the shade of a big rock, and Pengey kept him well supplied with fresh fish.

Lionel flew back and forth to the Brazil nut tree. He gathered the nuts and brought them back to the beach. He knew they would be flying over a lot of water. He knew that Pengey and Rufus could always find food in the ocean, but for him it was going to be a long haul.

At the end of that third day, when the temperature of the tropics had cooled off and the sea breezes brought a cooling mist onto the shore, our intrepid band of heroes gathered together to watch the sunset.

They all knew that tomorrow morning they would embark on their journey across the mighty Atlantic Ocean.

They all knew that sleep would be difficult that night.

Chapter 23

THE JOURNEY BEGINS

The morning slipped onto the little beach with a thick blanket of fog and cold wind. Pengey felt right at home, and Rufus wasn't exactly put off by the cooler weather.

Lionel, on the other hand, rather liked it when the temperature was closer to seventy-five or higher. This morning it was more like fifty-five, and with the thickness of the fog, visibility was less than a hundred feet in any direction.

Lionel looked at Rufus and said, "Now how am I supposed to take off with Pengey on my back in weather like this?"

Rufus said, "Beats me."

In the meantime, Pengey had been up and out, swimming around catching little squids and krill. He even caught an anchovy—yum, yum! He caught a bunch of the little fish, the kind Rufus liked, brought them up on shore, and dropped them in front of Rufus.

Rufus said, "Thanks." He gobbled down a fish and asked, "What do you think about leaving today? It's awfully foggy."

Pengey said, "I don't know the first thing about flying. In fact, I don't think any penguins can fly, not in the air at least. He pondered a moment and said proudly, "But underwater . . . we can fly underwater."

Lionel said, "What we're worried about is the fog and whether we can take off in it without crashing into anything."

Pengey pondered the options, "If you're really worried about it, then we should walk back up to the top of the cliff and take off from up there. That way we'll be above anything we could bump into."

Rufus said, "That, my dear Pengey, is a brilliant idea." And so off the threesome trudged up the side of the cliff. There were ancient walking trails cut into the slope, so it wasn't a particularly dangerous climb. Once they had huffed and puffed their way to the top, they were a little tired, but no one was prepared for what they saw.

They peeked over the top edge of the cliff. There, very close by, a circus had set up its tents. Dozens of humans were milling about preparing for the events of the day. Some were dressed in silly and colorful costumes; some were practicing balancing acts or juggling objects in the air.

One man was filling up brightly colored objects that he attached to long pieces of string. When he finished with one, he'd put it with the others floating beside his worktable.

Pengey was fascinated by all the activity and colorful sights around the tents. Lionel and Rufus stayed hidden below the edge of the cliff and wondered how to get onto the top without being seen by the humans.

Pengey wanted to go out and say hello to everyone, but Lionel convinced him that it was wiser to stay hidden, because this circus could be the one owned by the evil ringmaster.

And so they stayed hidden at the very top of the cliff and waited for the activity to die down. Still, they had to leave early in the morning because they hoped to pick up the jet stream and take it north. By flying securely in the jet stream, they might soar all the way across the Atlantic Ocean and beyond to the Caribbean Sea and maybe even make it to

Florida in the United States of America before nightfall.

They could hear the voice of the ringmaster calling out over the loudspeakers. He was summoning all the workers inside the circus tents.

At last the ridge top was devoid of humans. Pengey, Lionel, and Rufus, seeing the coast was clear, climbed up the last few steps, grateful that they hadn't been spotted.

They looked at the fog below. It was still very thick. The sun was shining, and a warm updraft meant that it would be fairly easy for Lionel to take off, even with the additional weight of Pengey and his backpack full of shelled Brazil nuts.

Pengey tied Wendy's red ribbon to Lionel's beak and the leather straps to Lionel's chest while Rufus kept a look out for bad guys.

When they were all ready for departure, Lionel said, "We're going to have to pump our wings as hard as we can in order to get into the jet stream. But once we do it will carry us along, and the flight should be relatively easy."

Pengey asked, "How do you know all these things?"

Lionel said, "I used to date a duck who lived summers out in Central Park. She made the north-to-south, roundtrip every year. She said it was a breeze."

Lionel cracked up and laughed and laughed. Rufus and Pengey looked at him as if he'd gone crazy. Lionel said, "A breeze. Get it? Duh! Jet stream? Breeze? Get it?"

Rufus rolled his eyes and chuckled. Pengey scratched his head because he still didn't get it.

Rufus looked over his shoulder and saw the ringmaster and the animal trainer running toward them. They ran so fast that they knocked over the man who was filling up the colorful objects attached to the long strings. Their faces bore looks of maniacal anger as they raced across the field. They were carrying a large net.

Rufus said, "If you're finished telling jokes, there's a couple of humans running this way, and they don't look too friendly."

Lionel looked over his shoulder and saw the threatening sight. He said, "Ready for takeoff, Pengey?"

"Ready as I'll ever be."

The ringmaster and the animal trainer were getting closer and shouting, "Stop! You're under arrest!"

Lionel looked at Rufus and said, "Ready?"

Rufus said, "Ready."

Pengey said, "We go on three." He wrapped his feet tightly around the leather straps, his flippers around the red ribbon, and shouted, "On my mark. One. Two. THREE!"

Just as the animal trainer tossed the net at them, our valiant threesome ran for the edge of the cliff.

Rufus lifted off immediately and soared high into the air.

Not realizing how much weight he was carrying, Lionel plunged over the edge and dropped like a stone. He flapped and flapped with his big and powerful wings, but he continued to fall.

Pengey held on for dear life as the columns of air rushed past him and tried to pull him away from the safety of Lionel's mighty back. But with his feet wrapped around the leather straps, he was securely attached.

Lionel forced his wings down with more power than he thought possible, but the free fall was all but unavoidable.

Finally he stiffened his wings as wide as they would go against a very strong and very warm updraft. They bellowed like sails in a windstorm, and he began to climb with the wind and move off into the atmosphere.

Lionel pumped his wings again and lifted higher and higher into the blue skies.

Rufus pulled alongside Lionel and Pengey, "What took you so long?'

Lionel said, "How'd you like to be carrying Pengey and his backpack?"

Rufus laughed and said, "No thanks."

Lionel said to Pengey, "I thought you only weighed four pounds."

Pengey said, "Well, I did eat a lot of krill, several squid, and an anchovy or two in the last few days."

Lionel said, "An anchovy or two?"

"Well, maybe three. Maybe I put on a little weight."

"A little? It feels like you put on a ton."

Pengey apologized in his most sincere voice. "I'm

terribly sorry. I didn't mean to gain weight. Will you be okay?"

Lionel said, "Sure, kid. I was just teasing you."

So Lionel and Rufus pumped their wings and flew higher and higher on the warm air current around the edges of the cliffs. But they weren't getting any closer, it seemed, to the jet stream.

Lionel said, "We'd better head inland. Maybe we can pick up the jet stream there."

And so they flew over the circus. They pumped their wings as hard as they could, but Lionel was having difficulty gaining altitude. Pengey and his backpack filled with Lionel's Brazil nuts simply weighed too much. Things were beginning to look pretty bleak.

Then off in the distance Pengey saw something rising high into the sky. It was made of many colors and it was quite large, but it was moving fast and rapidly gaining altitude.

He pointed at the brightly colored object, and Lionel flapped his wings for all he was worth to catch up to it. Rufus stayed right alongside of Lionel and Pengey.

Before long they caught up to an extremely large bundle of balloons, all tied together with individual strings. It was like a floating bouquet of flowers.

It was extremely difficult, but Lionel flapped very hard and pulled to within inches of the bouquet of balloons. Pengey reached out, grabbed the strings, and tied them to the leather straps around Lionel's chest. Rufus flew very close to Pengey, and Pengey tied a leather strap to Rufus's foot and the other end to Lionel's chest straps.

And up and away they went. The balloons were gaining altitude at an alarming rate. Up, up, up they went, the balloons pulling them along with ease.

After a twenty-minute ascent they must have hit the jet stream, because all of a sudden they were zooming along at an incredible rate of speed. They were so high that the forests, lakes, rivers, and the whole countryside of Brazil looked like a patchwork quilt.

They flew that way for five hours. It was almost effortless. They must have traveled over seven hundred miles. Then, almost without warning, the jet stream changed directions, and they were flying west instead of north.

Lionel recognized the directional change and yelled, "Pengey! Let go of the balloons!"

Pengey was confused by the order, but it sounded urgent, so he untied the balloons and the leather strap that held Rufus to Lionel and then let go of the balloons.

Lionel dove out of the jet stream, Rufus following directly behind him.

When they reached an altitude of about two hundred feet, they leveled out into smoother air. They also found that they could pick up thermal drafts along the northeastern coast of Venezuela.

Happily, the flight was proceeding even better than expected.

Chapter 24

THE VOLCANO

They flew along the coast of Venezuela. The contrasting temperatures of the cool Atlantic Ocean and the hot tropical landmass provided many long and welcome thermal updrafts. These updrafts caused a cushion of air to rise swiftly under Lionel and Rufus's wings, and it kept them aloft with very little effort.

So they zoomed along from thermal to thermal. They reached amazing speeds as they dove down from one thermal to the next. It was like being on a giant roller coaster in the sky.

Pengey was having a ball.

The ride on Lionel's back reminded him of the policeman on horseback at the airport in Rio. So he amused himself by pretending he was a policeman riding horseback, and the hours seemed to melt away.

Far below them, off the shoreline, many small boats were busy fishing in the tropical waters. Pengey wasn't afraid of the ocean because he was such a good swimmer, but he was deeply concerned about Lionel because he couldn't swim at all.

Our intrepid band of travelers was hungry, but they persevered with their flight plan. They flew along the coast and stayed with the warm thermals that moved them along so swiftly and effortlessly.

The day marched on virtually without incident. But after eight hours in the air they left the coastline of Venezuela and flew over the warmer waters of the Caribbean Sea.

Now the thermals completely vanished. They flew over the Caribbean at a steady speed. But both Lionel and Rufus had to continually flap their wings to stay airborne. The day was still warm but not too hot, which made for good travel weather. Lionel and Rufus had to work harder, but progress was steady.

Pengey noticed that, as hard as Lionel was working, they were slowly losing altitude, but he decided to keep it to himself because he didn't want to embarrass Lionel.

Still progress remained steady, and they flew further and further into the inner reaches of the Caribbean, not knowing where they could land. Out on the horizon Pengey could see an accumulation of mighty storm clouds.

He'd seen such a storm once before. That storm was so huge that it had wiped out his entire ice floe. He was afraid and rightfully so, because storms at sea can be very dangerous, indeed.

Lionel saw the storm as well, but he wasn't concerned because he knew it was traveling away from them toward the southeast, and they were heading due north.

They were very far out to sea, perhaps one hundred miles or so, but they had lost so much altitude that Pengey could see the whitecaps on the ocean below. Now they were only about fifty feet above the ocean, and Lionel had been straining severely for the last hour or so. Rufus was getting tired, too, but he flew alongside of Lionel and Pengey. He was a steady companion who was conserving his energy by not saying a word.

The sun was beginning to set, and they knew that they had to land soon or face the ocean at night. And that would mean that Lionel would have to learn to swim—not a likely thing for a parrot.

In the near distance Pengey could see land. It was just a tiny speck of land with a tall, strange-looking mountain in the middle of it.

Pengey leaned close to Lionel's ear and said, "How about that little island?"

Lionel nodded agreement and headed for landfall.

Ten minutes later Lionel, Rufus, and Pengey landed on top of an extinct volcano. There was tropical vegetation all around, but the sea was over a mile away.

Rufus lay next to Lionel on the ground, both breathing very hard; they were totally exhausted. Pengey opened his little backpack and gave Lionel some of the Brazil nut meats. Lionel gobbled them down gratefully and lay back down.

He huffed and puffed, "As soon as we can, we have to get into the safety of a tree. You can never tell what creatures and dangers may be lurking in these tropical forests."

Pengey asked in his most sincere voice, "If you please, Lionel, . . . exactly what kind of creatures are you referring to?"

Lionel rubbed his eyes and yawned and said, "Snakes, red-tail hawks, too, but mostly snakes. They're sorta slow, but they creep up on you and . . . well, I won't go into details. Just beware of the snakes, okay?"

Pengey and Rufus nodded agreement. They both seemed to be falling asleep. Pengey knew it was too early to go to sleep. He knew they had to find shelter and eat in order to have the energy to continue the trip in the morning.

He remembered the way that the policeman with the dog, Wolf, had talked to Wendy when he was taking her away to the airplane. So he said in his most commanding voice, "Listen up! There'll be no sleeping, not yet. Rufus, you fly down to the sea and catch us some fish."

Rufus slowly got up and brushed himself off. There was a stiff breeze coming up the side of the volcano, so he spread his wings and it lifted him into the air. He yawned and said, "You're right, Pengey. I'll be right back."

"Lionel, wake up." Pengey said sternly, "Rufus has gone to get us some food. You need to forage around for some berries so you can keep your strength up. I'll look for a tree for us to sleep in."

Lionel nodded agreement, yawned a sleepy yawn, and said, "Okay, okay. I suppose you're right." He shook his head and spread his wings against the stiff breeze and lifted off. He called out to Pengey. "Hold down the fort, kid. I'll be back in a jiffy."

Pengey confidently walked around the edge of the volcano's crater in search of a likely place to sleep.

Little did he know, but he was observed. He was at this very moment being hunted by a large snake called a red-bellied racer. The sneaky snake slithered silently through the steamy underbrush around the crater's edge.

Its plan was simple: it would catch Pengey and eat him, just like that. But he was a smart snake who was not taking any chances. He had also seen Lionel and Rufus, and if the three of them were together he might lose if a fight broke out.

The sinister snake bided his time and waited for Pengey to walk his way—then he would pounce on him.

Pengey was hungry, and when he was hungry he pondered his options. In his pondering, he thought that the other side of the volcano was prettier but that this side had a better view. There was an extremely large tree on the other side. This side had a big tree, too, but it seemed scrawny in comparison.

Of course, this side was a bit cooler and had a nice stiff breeze. The breeze would be a big advantage for takeoff in the morning. This side also had some very nice rocks, and Rufus seemed to be quite fond of rocks—so this side had a lot going for it, too.

Pengey, without knowing it, walked closer and closer to the venomous predator snake. He was quite close indeed and the snake was, in fact, ready to pounce on him.

But Pengey suddenly turned away, walked in the other direction, and pointed at a rather tall tree that was located on this side but slightly below, down the slope of the volcano.

"Hmmm. . . ," said Pengey, "I wonder if that tree would be tall enough?" He backed up and held his flippers up to frame the tree like a picture. He kept backing up toward the snake and the edge of the volcano, while still framing the tree with his flippers.

The sneaky snake waited until Pengey was almost on top of him. Then he sprang from his recoil and silently shot out from the bushes to pounce on Pengey.

As it flew toward him, Pengey looked at the snake as if he had all the time in the world, and said in a most casual tone of voice, "Snake." Then he nimbly jumped out of the snake's way as he hurled himself past Pengey at a frightful speed.

And the snake tumbled, THUD, BANG, CRASH, POW—screaming, Aaaahhhhh!!!!!—head-over-tail, all the way down into the mouth of the volcano, never to be seen again.

Just then Lionel flew back and shouted Pengey's name, but Pengey was busy looking over the edge of the volcano to see what had happened to the snake.

He got up, dusted off his feathers, and yelled out to Lionel, "Here I am, over here!"

Lionel flew over to where Pengey was standing on the very edge of the volcano. Lionel looked at the dirt on Pengey's feathers and said, "How'd you get so dirty?"

Pengey said, "Snake."

"Whadaya mean 'snake?' Didja see one?"

"Why yes, I did in fact see a snake."

Lionel backed up and looked at Pengey in a curious fashion, "How'd ya know it was a snake?"

Pengey said, "It looked like a stick but it could fly."

"Snake's can't fly," said Lionel.

Pengey pointed with his flipper into the mouth of the volcano and said, "Well, maybe they can and maybe they can't, but that snake was trying to fly."

"What snake?"

"The snake that's at the bottom of the volcano."

Lionel rolled his eyes and took Pengey under his wing and said in a solemn tone, "The day that snakes can fly I'll turn into a penguin."

Pengey said, "You make it sound like there's something wrong with being a penguin."

"No," said Lionel, "but there would be something very wrong if snakes could fly."

Just then Rufus flew up and landed on a little patch of grass. He dropped seven little fish from his beak and called out for Pengey.

Pengey trundled over to Rufus and said, "Is that for me?"

Rufus said, "Yeah! The fishing is great in this part of the world. I ate while I was down at the water. Help yourself, they're all yours."

So as the sun set, Pengey sat down on the grassy knoll and gobbled down the delicious little fish. Rufus kept watch, and Lionel scouted out the best tree for them to camp in for the night.

About a half hour later it was dark, and the threesome had snuggled into a nest that Lionel had built. They were extremely tired but happy, because the first leg of their journey had gone along quite smoothly, all in all.

Still, Rufus and Lionel took turns sleeping and keeping watch on the jungle floor below them—because one could never tell what dangers lurked, unseen, in these tropical forests.

Chapter 25

RAFAEL

Pengey slumbered well until the full moon popped up over the horizon. The moon was so bright it startled him back from sleep—or maybe it was the noise he thought he heard.

Pengey got up and walked across the thick branch to where Lionel was keeping a careful and vigilant watch.

Pengey said in a sleepy voice, "I can't sleep."

Lionel pressed his wing to his beak in a cautionary fashion and said, "Hush," and then he whispered, "Shhhh."

Pengey whispered back, "How come we have to whisper, there's no one around."

Lionel whispered even more softly, "That's just the problem. There's something out there."

Pengey enthusiastically popped his head over the edge of the branch and whispered, "Where? I don't see anyone."

Lionel pushed Pengey's head back from the edge of their branch and silently pointed to another branch lower on the tree. Then they both peeked over the edge.

The moonlight illuminated something long and low. It had a big head and a long tail and it moved slowly and effortlessly along the branch. It looked like a dragon.

Pengey quivered with fear of this unknown creature. The creature stopped moving, and after a short while it started to snore.

It snored quite loudly, in fact. It, whatever it was, was fast asleep.

Pengey wondered what the creature was, but Lionel made him go back to bed because they had to leave very early in the morning when the breeze off the Caribbean would be the strongest and offer the greatest lift to their takeoff. Pengey reluctantly walked back to the nest and snuggled down next to Rufus, who was also awake.

Rufus whispered, "What were you and Lionel talking about?"

Pengey whispered back, "There's a creature in the branches, and Lionel doesn't know what it is. He's quite concerned about it."

Rufus got up and walked over to Lionel, and they whispered something to each other, but the snoring of the creature had become very loud and they decided that there was no threat.

Rufus relieved Lionel from guard duty. Lionel walked back to the nest and tried to go to sleep. He slept uncomfortably, as did Pengey, because of the loud snoring and the intensely bright moonlight rather than because of any immanent threat.

Pengey tossed and turned and watched the stars overhead. He watched the moon and the creatures that flew across its shiny face. Lionel had explained that these creatures that flew at night were bats and that they ate insects and fruit. He explained that they were beneficial to the ecosystems of the small Caribbean islands.

So Lionel and Pengey just watched the bats fly across the face of the moon until Pengey fell back to sleep.

In the morning Pengey was up like a shot. He dashed to the spot where Lionel was keeping watch and where he had last seen the creature. He looked for it, but it was gone.

Pengey said, "Drat it! I wanted to see the creature."

Lionel said, "It must have left the tree some time before dawn." He stretched, yawned, and pointed with his wing. "Look, I've got to fill up on some of those berries over there. You should wake Rufus up so we can take off before the wind dies down."

And with that Lionel spread his wings and lifted off and away to some nearby berry bushes. Pengey walked back and woke Rufus up, but Rufus was a little grumpy because he hadn't slept well.

Rufus said, "W-what? Oh, it's you Pengey."

"Time to get up."

Rufus shook off his slumber. "Thanks. I didn't realize it was so late."

Pengey said, "I know you didn't sleep very well last night. That's why I thought you should sleep in. But Lionel wants to get an early start, so he told me to wake you up."

"He's right," said Rufus as he stretched and flapped his wings. "It's an awfully pretty day. I'll scoot down to the beach and get us some food. Will the same fish we had last night be okay?"

Pengey said, "Why, yes. Those were delicious."

Rufus spread his wings and took off on the updraft,

saying, "See you in a half hour, less if I'm lucky."

Pengey yelled out, "Good luck." And Rufus flew off to the shoreline.

It was too dangerous to leave the tree, and there wasn't much for him to do while he waited for Lionel and Rufus to return. So Pengey looked in his backpack. He took out Wendy's business card and the little laminated picture of her. He looked at the business card, but except for her name, he still didn't understand the words.

A tear was tumbling across his little beak, when all of a sudden, a voice came out of nowhere.

"I know exactly how you feel. I feel the same way most of the time myself."

Pengey looked around and saw that he was face to face with the monstrous-looking creature.

The monster said, "Buenos dias, Senor. Permit me to introduce myself. I am Rafael Miguel Xavier Roberto Constantino Morales Ortega. You can call me Rafael. I'm an iguana."

Pengey shrank back from the monster, which was, after all, only a gigantic iguana.

Rafael laughed shyly and said, "You needn't be afraid of me. I know I'm scary looking, but I'm really a very nice person, and I've never eaten anything but vegetables in my whole life."

Pengey was not convinced. After all, this was a fearsome-looking beast with long claws, a long green body, and things that stuck up off its head and back like pointy spikes.

Rafael smiled and said, "I saw you and your two friends hanging around up here in the tree last night. So I decided to come and visit, but I fell asleep before I got here."

Pengey was speechless and still terrified by the sight of Rafael.

Rafael laughed in an insecure manner and said, "It's okay if you don't like me. Most people think I'm ugly. I get picked on so much, I'm beginning to think it's true." He started to walk away, "Sorry to have bothered you. I guess I'll be going now. Adios."

The shock of surprise left Pengey's face, and he looked on this iguana, who called himself Rafael, with some compassion. He said, "Wait, don't go Mr. Rafael. I don't think you're ugly, you just scared me. You see, being from the South Pole and all I've never seen anyone like you before in my life."

Rafael said, "Aw, shucks . . . I didn't mean to scare you. Heck, I don't mean to scare anyone, but I can't help the way I look. Say, what are you, anyway? I've never seen anyone like you before."

Pengey bowed and said proudly, "I'm a penguin, an emperor penguin, in fact. Pengey Penguin's the name."

Rafael laughed and said, "You're kinda short for an

emperor, aren't you?"

Pengey said, "I am short in height, to be sure. But I'm big in many other ways—besides, I can talk Human."

Rafael was absolutely astonished, "You can talk Human? That's amazing, wait 'til I tell the gang. He stopped, thought deeply for a moment, and asked, "Do all penguins talk Human?"

Pengey scratched his head and said, "As far as I know, I'm the only penguin that has ever spoken Human."

Rafael said, "Wow, man! You are one cool penguin. I mean, what I mean to say is that—that is truly impressive."

Pengey bowed, smiled, and said, "Thank you very much. I'm very much impressed with you and your name. Could you say it again?"

Rafael repeated, "I am Rafael Miguel Xavier Roberto Constantino Morales Ortega. I'm an iguana."

Pengey said, "Wow! You must have the longest name in the whole wide world."

Rafael looked sheepishly away, and his cheeks blushed a little red, "No, it's just the way Spanish people do the name thing."

"What's Spanish?"

"People from the country of Spain. They settled these islands some three hundred years ago, and that's how come everything around sounds like it's from Spain."

Pengey and Rafael talked about Spain and its people

for quite a while. Pengey decided that he'd like to go to Spain sometime because Rafael made it sound like a very special place.

They talked about their moms and dads and found out that they were both eggs before they became real animals. It was most astonishing news to both Pengey and Rafael. They had become pretty good friends by the time Lionel got back.

When Lionel landed on the branch, he puffed up his chest and flapped his wings at Rafael.

Rafael backed away, for he was terribly afraid of Lionel's ferocious look.

Lionel yelled, "ARK!" and then he puffed out his chest and flapped his wings some more and yelled, "Stand back, you monster!"

Rafael trembled and cowered. He almost fell off the branch.

Pengey jumped in front of Lionel, waved his flippers, and yelled, "Stop! You're scaring him, Lionel. This is Rafael, he's an iguana. He's not a monster, he's my new friend."

Lionel was unsure because of Rafael's fierce look. He said, "He looks like a monster."

Rafael said in his embarrassed manner, "Thank you very much. That is, I'd like to think that I'm fierce but actually, I'm really a fraidy-cat."

Pengey said, most enthusiastically, "Yeah, see? He's a fraidy-cat. But he's also a really nice person, and he knows all about Spain. You see? We got to be friends while you were out gathering your breakfast."

Lionel shook his head and said, "Any friend of Pengey's is a friend of mine."

And so Lionel and Rafael and Pengey sat on the branch and discussed what life was like on the tiny island while they waited for Rufus to get back.

The sight of Rafael terrified Rufus, and he wouldn't land. But constant persuasion from both Lionel and Pengey convinced him that Rafael wouldn't eat him.

As soon as he landed, Rufus dropped some of the little fish for Pengey, who gobbled them down and thanked Rufus most prodigiously.

The four mismatched friends spent the next fifteen minutes discussing the best route to New York City. Rafael was generally confused about the whole process of travel, but he was pretty sure New York was north. Lionel, Rufus, and Pengey didn't want to make Rafael feel bad, so they let him think that he had shown them the way.

It was time to go, and so Pengey climbed up on top of Lionel's back and grabbed hold of Wendy's red ribbon. The sea breeze was at its peak, and so with a sad farewell Pengey, Rufus, and Lionel said good-bye to Rafael.

They took off and headed due north. Pengey waved his flipper and Rafael waved good-bye. He felt proud to have met Pengey and the others. Rafael wiped some tears from his eyes as he watched his new friends fly away. He kept the hope that someday he would get to see them all again.

Then he walked away to find some vegetables for breakfast.

Chapter 26

THE WRATH OF THE SEA

The day was warming up quickly, and as a result there wasn't much of a thermal draft once they got offshore of the tiny island.

This was the sixth day of the journey, and even though they hadn't slept well they were all in high spirits because they felt they were getting closer to New York City. They knew that many miles and many dangers lay ahead, but they were undaunted by the enormous task that lay before them.

They flew as high as they could go, but neither Rufus nor Lionel had the strength to get into the jet stream. Still, the tailwind was quite strong at that altitude, so flight wasn't as laborious as it might have been.

And so they plodded along at a steady pace. Rufus flew directly beside Lionel. Pengey sang made-up songs to keep things as cheerful as possible in what was surely an awesome display of courage and conviction.

The day and the miles marched on. They flew over many small islands that looked very much like the one they had camped on last night. On and around these islands Pengey could see that life was flourishing. He saw little towns with their brightly painted buildings and little fishing boats that seemed to scurry around in the shallow waters off the island coastlines.

They wanted to land and have something to eat, but their mission was to keep on course. They bore on, straight ahead into their adventure, keeping stout faith that all would be well and that no harm would come to them.

By late afternoon it was getting cloudy. The change was gradual to be sure, but there seemed to be no way around the dark clouds that were approaching.

It was very dark now, and they agreed that it might be best to find someplace to wait out what was sure to be a terrible storm.

The wind suddenly became very strong and they were blown in all directions. In an instant it became all but unmanageable for Lionel and Rufus to maintain altitude. Pengey had to hold on tighter than ever because the winds were so strong that they threatened to push him off Lionel's back. He wrapped his feet tighter in the leather straps and rode with the turbulence.

They had to get out of the storm. It started raining hard, and Lionel's feathers were not waterproof. It was getting to be an extreme struggle for him. As hard as he flapped, he was losing altitude at an uncontrollable rate.

Down and down they went. The rain and wind buffeted our valiant heroes. Lionel's wings were drenched, and he was rapidly falling.

They were down close to the water by now, and the rain and wind pummeled them from all directions. The sudden and mighty storm was relentless.

At last Lionel could fly no more. He looked all around him, but there was no land in sight. He flapped as hard as he could, but it was no use, and he and Pengey fell into the churning and turbulent waters of the Caribbean.

Pengey immediately jumped off of Lionel's back. He swam around and took the red ribbon off Lionel's beak and stuffed it quickly into his backpack.

Lionel couldn't swim, and his feathers were so wet he began to sink into the churning water. He looked at Pengey and Rufus and said, "I guess I'm done for. I can't fly in this weather, and I don't know how to swim. My feathers are so wet I don't think I'll be able to float much longer." The angry waves rose and fell and crashed all around them and only Lionel's head remained above the water.

He said, "Be brave, you two. I know you're going to make it to New York." And with a last desperate gulp of air Lionel slipped beneath the wild and unforgiving waves.

Pengey quickly tossed the backpack to Rufus. He had to yell to be heard above the din of the storm. "Hold that and don't let anything happen to it!" he shouted.

Rufus grabbed the backpack as he floated on the water and yelled, "Where are you going?"

But there was not a second to lose, so Pengey dove as fast as his little flippers would go into the darkened sea of calamity.

As dark as it was underwater, Pengey could see fairly well. He could see the vague outline of Lionel falling deeper and deeper into the merciless sea. He dove for all he was worth toward Lionel.

Rufus floated on the storm-tossed surface. His waterproof feathers kept him dry enough to float. But Pengey had been underwater for almost a minute, and he knew that he didn't have enough air in his little lungs to help Lionel breathe.

Rufus was beginning to think all was lost. He thought Pengey was doomed in his effort to help Lionel. He looked at Pengey's backpack and remembered his words, "Don't let anything happen to this."

A sad tear fell from Rufus's eye. He figured he would wait out the storm and fly to a small island to recuperate, but he was so sad at the loss of his friends that he was beside himself with grief.

But then an amazing thing happened. Lionel's head slowly broke the surface of the water.

He coughed and spit and sucked in huge gulps of air. He was having a hard time controlling his coughing because he had swallowed so much water.

Rufus panicked when he heard Lionel cough. He yelled, "Where's Pengey?"

Lionel couldn't stop coughing, so he pointed into the water. Finally he said, "He's right underneath me."

Rufus swam to Lionel and patted him on the back. More water came out of Lionel's beak, and he coughed a few more times.

Rufus gave Pengey's backpack to Lionel and said, "Don't let anything happen to this." Lionel took the backpack in his beak, and Rufus dove under water. And there, lo and behold, was Pengey. He had his head buried in Lionel's tummy. He was holding his breath and flapping his flippers as fast and as hard as he could.

Rufus could only hold his breath for a little less than a minute, so he popped back up to the surface.

Rufus said, "Pengey's keeping you afloat."

Lionel said, "I know! Believe me, I know."

Rufus was in a panic, "Well, that's not going to work,"

he said. "He's got to breathe at some point. I mean his little flippers are going a mile a minute down there. He's using up his oxygen at a very fast rate."

Lionel said, "I'm grateful for what he's doing, but I don't want him to die because of me. Still, life is precious. Maybe he has a plan."

Rufus swiftly dove back underwater and used sign language to communicate with Pengey. Pengey signaled to Rufus to go and get some air and come right back. Rufus zoomed up to the surface of the water, grabbed a big gulp of air, and dove back down to Pengey.

Pengey motioned to Rufus to get under Lionel. He showed him how to place his head in Lionel's belly and flap his wings to keep him afloat. Rufus got the idea right away, and Pengey raced for the surface.

Lionel was beside himself when Pengey popped out from the murky water. Pengey breathed very deeply many times to fill his little lungs to the very top.

Pengey gasped, "Rufus has you now, but he can't hold his breath very long. I'll bonk you with my flipper when I need to breathe again, and you can send Rufus down." With that Pengey dove into the turbulence to relieve Rufus.

And so it went all the rest of the day.

Little Pengey would stay underwater as long as he could, then Rufus would swim down to relieve him. But the day and the relentless storm were also long, and Pengey was getting tired. He couldn't stay underwater for more than a few minutes now, and Rufus could only stay for twenty seconds or less.

Miraculously, the rain stopped just as suddenly as it had

started. It was still very foggy, but the wind had also dissipated.

Lionel immediately flapped his wings to dry them off. As the water drained off his wings, he found that he could lift himself a little above the waves. But his body feathers were so wet it made takeoff quite impossible.

The three of them were exhausted. Pengey and Rufus floated on the surface of the water. Lionel, having been buoyed up for all those stormy hours, now had energy to save himself. He was flapping his wings enough to stay afloat, and that gave Pengey and Rufus some much-needed rest.

Still another hour went by, and as tired as Pengey was, he had to dive under Lionel again because the parrot's wings were still too wet, and he was sinking again.

Hour after lonely hour, Pengey and Rufus exchanged places and kept Lionel afloat. The sun was starting to set when Pengey popped his head out before what he knew would be the last time he could go under. He huffed and puffed and said, "I'm sorry, Lionel, but . . . " Then he screamed, "Look out!!!"

There above them, slipping out of a fog bank, was a very large ship. Someone from the ship yelled, "Ahoy!"

Pengey didn't know what *ahoy* meant, but it sounded cool, so he yelled out, "Ahoy!"

Rufus popped out of the water, and Lionel flapped his wings for all he was worth.

On the ship a young man said to an older man, "Sir! We seem to have encountered some castaway animals. One of them is a penguin who appears to speak English."

The older man said, "Well then, let's give them a leg

up, shall we?"

There was much yelling and scurrying around on the big ship, and in the next moment or two a small boat pulled up along side our dynamic threesome.

Lionel was sinking fast. Pengey took his final dive and pushed hard against Lionel's tummy. Rufus grabbed the backpack in his beak and pulled on it as Lionel bit into its other end. Lionel's beak was just above the water line—breathing was torturous.

Sailors dressed in blue uniforms and little blue caps raced against time to pull Lionel from the water. Next they pulled out Rufus, and at last they reached Pengey, who was clutching onto his little backpack.

The sailors put Pengey down on the floor of the boat, and he bowed very deeply and cooed his most earnest coo.

Pengey said in Human, "Thank you very much."

The sailors passed amused and amazed glances among themselves. One sailor put out his hand and shook Pengey's flipper.

The sailor said, "Pas de quoi, Monsieur Penguin. It means 'You're welcome'."

Pengey looked curiously at the sailor who had just spoken and said, "Pas de quoi?"

The sailor laughed and said, "It is French, Monsieur Penguin . . . my home language."

Pengey said, " New York . . . home."

"Oui, Monsieur Penguin, New York is your home."

The sailor who had spoken covered our heroes with warm, dry blankets while the other sailors rowed the lifeboat back to the ship.

Chapter 27

A LITTLE TIME TO REST

The ship was named *Marie Cousteau,* and it sailed out of Paris, France. It housed a crew and officers totaling thirty-five men and women. Some worked on the engines, others in the kitchen, some did the cleaning, and still others were in charge of the day-to-day navigation and actual piloting of the huge ocean-going craft.

There were also scientists on board who used the ship as a floating laboratory to study the weather. The scientists and officers of the ship were from many countries—a sort of international team of weather explorers.

Pengey, Lionel, and Rufus were given the royal treatment. Everyone on board ship was at once friendly and fascinated by the valiant threesome.

Jean, the sailor who led the rescue team, brought Pengey, Lionel, and Rufus to their quarters. Lionel was perched on his arm, Rufus was perched on his shoulder, but Pengey was cradled in his arms, still clutching his backpack and, one might add, at least half asleep.

In each area of the room the sailors had prepared accommodations for our fantastic three. In one corner was a stand of sorts. It had a horizontal pole on which Lionel could perch and sleep for the night.

In another corner there was a small space that looked like a tiny cave. It was made out of cardboard and filled with soft tissues. It was perfect for Rufus to back into and sleep the night away.

In the middle of the room there was a low bed, really just a small mattress and a little pillow. There was even a little blanket just big enough to cover Pengey.

Jean put Lionel on his perch. Lionel said, "Ark! Oh, my goodness." Then he put his head under his wing and went right to sleep.

Rufus flew down to his little cave and got right inside of it, then snuggled under his wing and went to sleep.

Jean walked over and knelt at Pengey's bed. He laid Pengey on it and petted his little head.

The sailor said, "You are very brave, Monsieur Penguin. I wonder, do you have a name?"

Pengey said, "Pengey."

The sailor said, "My name is Jean. It means John."

Pengey said, "Jean."

Jean smiled and said, "Merci, Monsieur Pengey. It means thank you."

Pengey said, "Merci, Monsieur Jean."

"The captain will wish to speak to you in the morning, Monsieur Pengey," said Jean, "but now you must sleep. Yes? Oui?"

Pengey looked at the sailor, smiled as only Pengey could smile, and said, "Oui, Monsieur."

"Do you wish to have a blanket, Monsieur Pengey?"

Pengey smiled and said, "Bankey."

Jean smiled again and tucked Pengey under the blanket. Pengey closed his eyes and put his flipper up and over them. He was asleep in an instant.

Jean thought he could see little z's coming out of Pengey's head. He rubbed his eyes but, when he looked again, the little z's were still there. So he stood up, tiptoed out of the room, and silently closed the door.

It was obvious to Jean as well to everyone else on board that something extraordinary had happened that day. They knew without knowing the details; they knew it in their heart of hearts.

They knew too that these little friends needed all the comfort and protection they could give them for as long as they needed it.

And so the ship cruised along on the now glassy smooth waters of the Caribbean. It cruised throughout the night and headed due north, toward the mainland of the United States of America.

Chapter 28

MORNING

By the time morning rolled around the *Marie Cousteau* had navigated some two hundred miles of the Caribbean Sea.

A bright and happy sun poured through the little round windows, called "portholes," built into the side of the ship. But our weary band of travelers slept on until it was almost ten o'clock.

Jean walked into the suite in which Pengey, Lionel, and Rufus were sleeping. He carried a wicker basket filled with fresh fruit and shelled nuts and little fish of all kinds. There were anchovies and sardines and even some tiny squid.

Lionel took his head out from under his wing, and Rufus did the same.

Pengey, on the other hand, snuggled deeper under his bankey.

Jean hooked a tin bowl onto Lionel's perch and filled it with Lionel's favorite nuts and fresh fruit. Lionel wasted no time in gobbling down the tasty treats.

Jean stooped down to Rufus's cubbyhole, put down a plate, and filled it with scrumptious little fish. Rufus climbed out of his cubbyhole and looked at Jean in an appreciative manner, then started to gobble down the little fish.

Pengey stirred, and so Jean approached his bed carrying the breakfast basket. He sat down very close to Pengey and pushed the basket closer to him. Pengey's eyes were still closed, but his little beak moved toward the basket as he sniffed the air.

Jean said, "Bonjour, Monsieur Pengey."

Pengey kicked off the blanket, rubbed his eyes, and yawned. He stretched and sniffed some more. He looked at Jean and smiled his Penguin smile and said, "Bonjour, Monsieur Jean."

Hearing Pengey speak French and say his name was too much for Jean, and he laughed and laughed. Pengey didn't know what to make of the laughter, so he started to laugh, too.

It seemed funny to Rufus and tickled Lionel's fancy as well. And there they sat, Pengey, Jean, Lionel, and Rufus, laughing their collective heads off.

Jean dried a happy tear from his eye and said, "You are a very special penguin, Monsieur Pengey. Do you belong to someone as special as you?"

Pengey opened his backpack, took out Wendy's business card, and passed it to Jean, who read it out loud.

Pengey gulped down another tasty fish. He looked at Jean, scratched his sleepy head with his flipper, and said, "Wendy, home."

Pengey pulled Wendy's picture out of his backpack, passed it to Jean, and said, "Wendy."

Jean raised an eyebrow when he gazed on the photo of Wendy. She was very pretty and had a kind look to her, a sort of inner beauty that showed through even in a photograph. He looked at Pengey and said, "May I keep these, Monsieur?"

Pengey ate another fish and said, "Wendy, home."

Jean didn't understand Pengey's comment, so he started to stand up with the card and the photo. Pengey cooed long and low, and when Jean looked at him, Pengey was shaking his head no.

Jean put the photo and card back in Pengey's backpack and said in his most humble tone of voice, "I am sorry, Monsieur. I did not mean to offend you." Pengey realized that Jean was being polite, so he stood up and bowed and cooed.

Jean smiled and said, "The captain would like to see you in one half hour. I will leave the door open for you, okay?"

Lionel said, "Ark! Captain, half hour."

Pengey continued to bow, and Jean left the room with smile on his face.

When Lionel and Pengey looked at Rufus he had fallen back to sleep.

So Lionel flew down to Pengey, and they ambled over to Rufus and stood there beside him wondering if they should wake him up. After all, if it weren't for Rufus, Lionel would probably have been taken by the angry sea. But then again if it weren't for Lionel, Pengey would still be the prisoner of the mad scientist. And if it weren't for their friendship, who knows what might have happened to any of them?

So without further delay Pengey started parading around, clapping his flippers and singing a happy song, and Lionel joined in. They were quite loud, and Rufus was awake in no time at all. He said, "All right you guys. Gee, a fella can't even get a couple of extra winks without you bustin' his beak."

Pengey said, "Come on, grumpy face. We have to go and see the captain."

Rufus said, "Okay, okay, but I hope they serve lunch pretty soon. I'm starved."

Chapter 29

THE HEROES' REWARD

The entire crew, including the captain, first mate, and the weather scientists, were up on deck preparing for a new experiment, and everyone was extremely busy.

Jean reported to the captain with a snappy salute.

The captain said in French, "At ease, Jean. What have you to report?"

Jean said, "I have been below, sir. I have found the travelers we rescued to be in excellent spirits."

The captain asked, "Have they eaten well?"

Jean replied, "Yes, sir. They all had hearty appetites and seem to be no worse for the wear and tear they went through during the squall."

The captain looked proud of himself and of Jean. "We saved some very special souls yesterday, Jean," he said. "When will they be coming up on deck?"

Jean replied, "I told the young penguin that you were eager to see him. He seems to understand English perfectly." He cleared his throat and said, "In fact, sir, he's picked up a little French since yesterday."

The captain looked at Jean curiously and said, "A-a little French? Most unusual."

Meanwhile back in Pengey's room, he and Lionel and Rufus were just leaving and trying to find their way to the upper deck. They wandered through the open doorway and entered the hall, where there were many doors, all closed.

They walked down the hallway and saw an open door, walked through it, and entered a large room with many big machines that made a lot of noise and looked sort of like the ones in the mad scientist's laboratory.

Claude, a big man in a sweaty undershirt and pants, approached the dynamic three and said in a gruff tone, "Hey! You there! Can't you read?" He pointed to a sign that said, "Engine Room"—"Authorized Personnel Only." He looked at Pengey and spoke firmly, "You don't look like authorized personnel to me."

Pengey looked curiously at Claude and said, "Captain?"

Claude looked closely at Lionel, Rufus, and Pengey and laughed, "No, I'm not the captain. He's up on the main deck." He pointed down the hallway and said, "And no matter how brave you were at sea, I don't want you three in my engine room. It's too easy to hurt yourselves in here. Now, you go on, the captain's just down the hall and up those stairs."

Lionel and Rufus walked toward the staircase, while Pengey backed away, bowing to Claude and saying, "Thank you very much."

Claude was taken by Pengey's manners, so he bowed back to Pengey but remained firm. "Yes, yes, yes. Now off with you. The captain is waiting." He smiled inwardly, went back into his engine room, and closed the door. Pengey, Lionel, and Rufus ambled down the hallway to a set of stairs.

But just down the hallway and beyond an open door the emotional voice of a woman called out in despair, while other voices, men's voices, sounded alternately threatening or cool and collected.

Pengey decided to investigate and see if he could help. Rufus and Lionel followed the brave little penguin, and they all entered the ship's lounge. In the corner stood a big-screen TV playing an old black-and-white movie.

A young sailor named Pierre was sitting on a sofa watching the movie. He turned around and saw our three heroes enter. Pengey had a most curious look on his face.

Pierre said, "Oh, hi guys. Don't worry, it's just a movie."

Pengey looked a little confused and said, "Movie?" and he watched some more.

Pierre explained how a private detective named "Nick Sloan" was very cool and collected, and even though he didn't have the best of manners, he was the good guy.

Pierre said that one of the bad guys was a bad policeman and that he had kidnapped the pretty girl. He went on to explain that Nick Sloan was working with the good policemen and trying to save the lady in distress.

Pengey decided on the spot that he would be a private eye. And when he was a private eye that he would be known as Pengey Sloan. Maybe he could find a hat and a tie like Nick Sloan's in New York City. It was all very reasonable to Pengey, quite simple and direct. If he were a private eye it would be easy to find Wendy.

Pierre asked, "Are you guys coming in to watch the movie, or are you just hanging out?"

Pengey pointed toward the stairs and said, "Captain."

Pierre said, "Yes! The captain's upstairs on the main deck."

Pengey bowed to Pierre, and our little threesome wandered over and started to climb the stairs.

Meanwhile up on deck, Jean was still briefing the captain on the situation, while the scientists were hard at work putting the finishing touches on their experiment. Jean said, "I'm sorry, Captain, but I do not think he understands the concept of time, that is, time beyond the normal instincts of a penguin his age. It also seems that he has a home in New York City."

The captain responded in disbelieving fashion, "New York City! Why he looks to be less than a year old."

Jean said, "Yes, sir! That much is true, but, in his backpack . . ."

The captain cut Jean off and said in a most astonished tone, "He has a backpack?"

"Yes, sir. He keeps nuts in it for the parrot but he has the business card and the photograph of a young woman who is a filmmaker and lives in New York. He calls her Wendy."

The captain said, "Such a strange set of anomalies."

"How's that, sir?"

The captain said, "A penguin that speaks English. A puffin lost at sea thousands of miles from his northern home, and a parrot who is flying to North America instead of South America. It's all very strange; perhaps it has something to do with global warming."

Jean snapped to attention and said, "Sir! Here they come."

The captain turned and watched Pengey poke his little head out of the doorway and look around in a sheepish fashion.

Jean called out, "Ah, Monsieur Pengey!" He motioned with his hand, "Come, come . . . Don't be shy."

But Pengey stayed in the doorway with his head peeking out and his little black eyes filled with wonder at the size of the ship and the amount of activity on its deck.

Rufus and Lionel stepped out onto the deck and looked around.

The scientists and others working on deck stopped what they were doing and watched in silence as Pengey took his first meek step toward the deck.

Then without warning they simultaneously broke out in applause. Lionel and Rufus backed away from Pengey, puffed up their chests, and joined in the general spirit of welcome for the hero on board.

The ruckus of the applause scared Pengey, so he ducked back away from the doorway. But Lionel motioned to him with his wing and said in animal talk, "It's okay, kid, all this noise is for you." Pengey was still unsure, and so Lionel coaxed him again, "Come on kid, this is what is known as 'a hero's welcome.'" Pengey stepped shyly onto the deck.

Lionel said, "Will ya come on, these people think you're great." He walked up to Pengey, winked at him, and whispered, "I think you're great, too."

Pengey looked at all the smiling faces of the people who stood by admiringly and whose applause continued to fill the air. He looked into the faces of Lionel and Rufus and saw the pride they had in their friendship with him.

He looked at Jean and the captain who, like all the others, stared in admiration at the brave little penguin while they smiled and clapped their hands.

Pengey started to bow. He turned slowly toward his well-wishers and bowed solemnly to each of them. He looked at Jean and the captain and bowed and cooed in his most formal manner. They returned the bow, and Jean motioned to Pengey to come closer.

Pengey shyly approached the captain and Jean. Jean stooped down to Pengey and said, "Bonjour, Monsieur Pengey."

Pengey bowed and said, "Bonjour, Jean."

Jean put the palm of his hand out to Pengey and asked, "May I lift you up?"

Pengey nodded affirmatively and stepped delicately onto Jean's hand. Jean lifted Pengey up for everyone to see him. As the applause died down, the captain held up his hand and asked for silence.

In the quiet of that moment the captain made a speech, "Monsieur Pengey, we are only human beings, and we do not know what you and your comrades experienced during yesterday's awful storm. But we know that without you, one of your brave companions would have been lost to the sea.

And so, my dear Monsieur Pengey le Debonair, to honor the miracles you orchestrated in the defense of the lives of your friends, I award you the Golden Feather to honor your most valiant deeds in the face of great adversity and without regard for your own life."

Pengey bowed to the captain, and the captain placed a beautiful red, white, and blue ribbon around Pengey's neck. In the center of the ribbon was pinned a little gold feather that now decorated Pengey's chest. Pengey bowed again and said, "Thank you very much, Monsieur Captain."

Everyone applauded again, but the captain held up his hands for silence. He turned his attention to Rufus and said, "And to you my brave puffin, I award you the Purple Ribbon of Honor. It represents not only your conviction but also the passion you must have had to have come so far on your valiant journey."

And with that Rufus flew up and perched on Jean's shoulder. The Captain placed a beautiful purple ribbon with a silver button around Rufus's neck.

They applauded, but again the captain called for silence. He turned his attention to Lionel and said, "And to the parrot we award the Wings of the Aviator, for we know without a doubt that it is your willingness and hearty spirit that allowed Monsieur Pengey to undertake his voyage."

Lionel flew up and landed on Jean's outstretched arm. The captain placed a yellow ribbon with a clasp of silver aviator wings over Lionel's neck.

Lionel bowed and said, "Ark! Oh my goodness," as everyone applauded and smiled.

Jean put the intrepid threesome on the deck where they proudly listened to more applause and whispers of greatness.

The captain again held up his hand, and again there was silence as he said, "Monsieur Pengey le Debonair, you are an inspiration to all of us, and we consider you to be a National Treasure. Would you be so kind as to let us take you home, back to France, with us?"

Pengey turned and bowed to everyone. He looked at the captain, bowed, and said in his tiny voice, " Wendy. New York . . . home."

The captain bowed respectfully to Pengey. He pointed east and said, "France is that way."

Then the Captain pointed due north and said, "New York City."

Pengey pointed his flipper toward New York City, and his tiny voice repeated, "Wendy, home."

The captain smiled and said, "Is there anything else we can do for you and your friends?"

Pengey looked toward the back of the ship and there, in the middle of the deck and in the middle of a rather significant scientific experiment, stood a gigantic weather balloon. Pengey pointed at the balloon with his little flipper and said, "Balloon? New York?"

Everyone thought that this was one clever little penguin.

And so it was that the crew fixed a large wicker basket to the bottom of the giant weather balloon, and before long Lionel, Rufus, and Pengey were placed on board the basket along with Pengey's backpack and an ample supply of fresh fish, nuts, and fruit.

The crew readied the balloon for liftoff.

Chapter 30

BALLOONING TO AMERICA

The entire crew gathered around the wicker basket and the weather balloon. A little sign pinned to the side of the basket read, "The Penguin Express."

Pengey bowed to everyone as they cheered and applauded. He stepped to the edge of the wicker basket and held up his flipper in the same manner as the captain had held up his hand.

The crowd fell silent as Pengey bowed and cooed in his most respectful way. "Thank you very much," he said.

The gathering became so still you could have heard a pin drop.

Pengey continued in very broken English, "You are good. I, me, go home now. Me come back. Thank you to help Pengey." Pengey turned to all those who were watching, bowed, and smiled and cooed in his most sincere and humble manner. They applauded and smiled in return.

The captain saluted Pengey and asked, "Are you ready for your departure, Monsieur Pengey?

Pengey looked at the captain, returned a snappy salute and said, "Oui, Captain, ready.

The captain said, "One moment, Monsieur." He looked at Jean and asked, "Is everything properly prepared?"

Jean saluted the captain. "Yes, sir. The winds aloft are headed due north. I have the balloon set for twenty thousand feet."

The captain said, "It should catch the edge of the jet stream nicely."

Jean approached the basket and said to Pengey, "Here is an extra blanket in case any of you get cold." He pointed to the lining of the basket and said, "The basket is lined with a natural cellulose. It will protect you from the high winds aloft."

Jean pointed to and pulled on some heavy-duty cord that was lashed onto the side of the basket. He said "These are for you to hold on to if the ride gets bumpy, okay?"

Pengey, Lionel, and Rufus nodded agreement.

Jean pointed to another long, heavy-duty cord that connected the enormous weather balloon to the wicker basket. He said, "When you get to New York, pull on this cord and the balloon will deflate."

Pengey looked confused.

Jean said as he tugged lightly on the cord, "New York. Balloon stop."

Pengey still looked confused.

Lionel said to Pengey in animal talk, "What he's trying to say is that when we get over The Big Apple, we pull that thing and the balloon will start to fall."

Pengey looked at Jean and nodded his understanding.

Jean said, "Now you three hold on tight. This balloon is going to go up really fast. When you hit the jet stream, you will be going very, very fast but with any luck, you'll be over New York City before nighttime, around when the sun is setting."

Pengey looked confused.

Jean said, "New York. Wendy. Sun sleeping."

Pengey smiled and bowed and put out his flipper. Jean took Pengey's flipper in his two fingers and shook it. Jean turned to the captain and said, "Ready for castoff, sir."

"Very well, let her go."

Jean approached the basket and said, "Au revoir, my little friend."

Pengey snapped a salute and said, "Au revoir, Jean."

Jean let go of the rope binding the weather balloon to the ship. The balloon rose very quickly. Everyone waved and cheered.

Pengey cooed his longest coo and smiled as only he knew how, and he waved good-bye.

Within a matter of seconds the balloon rose high into the air, and the ship looked like a toy boat on the water below.

From the deck of the ship Jean kept watch until the balloon had disappeared into the atmosphere. When it was completely gone from his sight, he raced into the radar room.

The radar man turned to Jean as he entered and said, "I have your balloon on my radar scope, and she is on course at twenty thousand feet, traveling at one-hundred-and-twenty knots."

Jean breathed a huge sigh of relief, thanked the radar man, and went back to his scientific work.

Meanwhile, aboard the weather balloon, Pengey, Lionel, and Rufus were holding on to the thick strings lashed into the sides of the basket. The balloon had caught a very fast moving current of air and was traveling seamlessly along with it.

The air rushed passed them. The wind was very strong, so they all ducked down below the rim of the basket and let the air pass over their heads.

Soon Lionel snuggled under the blanket and went to sleep. Rufus tucked his head under his wing, and he went to sleep, too.

Pengey was in a quandary, which confused him, and when Pengey got confused he pondered his options.

A quick peek over the edge of the basket confirmed that they were indeed very high above the earth. He could see many cloud formations and the curve of the earth beneath them. Indeed the entire tapestry of the earth's landmass, its lakes and rivers and oceans, was clearly visible. This caused Pengey great concern; after all, he had never seen New York City. In fact he had never even been in any city—he had just seen them from a distance. He wondered if Lionel would remember New York when they got there.

It was going to be a long flight, but Pengey didn't understand the concept of time outside of what a young penguin his age might understand from experience.

He decided that it was important not to miss anything, so he kept watch and peeked over the side of the basket frequently. But there was no sign of New York City.

The sun was warm and the balloon was moving at a great speed. It was smooth and effortless. After about an hour, Pengey snuggled under the blanket next to Lionel and Rufus and fell asleep. The balloon, still caught in the jet stream, raced on toward New York.

Chapter 31

SMOOTH SAILING

The trip was so smooth that they slept most of the way. But somehow, as if by some internal alarm clock, everyone woke up at the same time.

Pengey looked over the side of the basket and could see that they had descended quite a bit. He could make out roads and buildings. There were many buildings; in fact, so many that he thought that they might already be in New York.

Pengey said, "Look Lionel, we're in New York."

Lionel chomped down on a Brazil nut and said, "Relax kid. I'll let you know when we get there."

Pengey looked confused, "How will you know?"

Lionel said, "Trust me, Pengey. Once you've seen New York City you never forget her."

It may have had something to do with the jet stream at that altitude, but the balloon-powered basket was now only going about seventy miles per hour.

Forest after forest, river after river, farm after farm, lake after lake, and village after village passed under them. When they got to another city Pengey would look hopefully at Lionel, who would peek over the edge of the basket and shake his head no.

The sun was beginning to set and the number of buildings passing beneath them was uncountable. Still Lionel shook his head no, and the balloon sailed on.

The sun was dipping below the horizon. It looked like a fireball, and it turned the sky into a wash of deep oranges and reds that faded in time into deep reddish purple, to indigo blue, and finally into the black of night.

Off in the distance Pengey could see some very tall buildings. It was strange to see something so tall from that high in the sky.

Pengey shook Lionel and looked hopefully at him. Lionel stretched and yawned and looked over the basket's edge.

Lionel said, "Hey Rufus, wake up. This is our stop."

Pengey said, "At last."

Rufus said, "Gee, I haven't slept this good in months."

Pengey, Rufus, and Lionel ate until they were full, then readied for the final approach. Pengey set about preparing Lionel for the descent. He put all their ribbons and awards in his backpack. He and Rufus tied the leather straps to Lionel's chest, and then they put Wendy's red ribbon around Lionel's beak.

Pengey slipped his backpack over his flippers, climbed up on Lionel's back, and tucked his feet under the leather straps.

Lionel and Rufus each gave their wings a little workout in preparation for when the balloon would deflate. They nodded to each other in silent agreement.

Lionel looked at Pengey and said, "Ready?"

"Ready."

Lionel said, "Pull the rip cord."

Pengey grabbed the cord with his beak and pulled, and the balloon began to deflate.

Rufus jumped over the edge of the basket and took flight.

Lionel jumped onto the edge of the basket and spread his huge wings. The updraft caught him just right, and he lifted off and away and joined up with Rufus as they headed for the island of Manhattan and the city called New York, now only about twenty miles away.

Pengey was having a ball. He liked riding on Lionel's back much more than riding in the basket. Here he was out in the open, and he could feel the wind on his face and Lionel's powerful muscles flapping his huge wings.

It was dark by now, and the enormously tall and brightly lit buildings were getting closer and closer.

Pengey had never seen anything like New York City. What would it be like trying to find Wendy in such a big place?

"How will we find Wendy?" he asked.

Lionel said, "We'll camp in Central Park for the night and find her in the morning. Don't worry so much, kid. It'll be a cinch."

And so land they did in a beautiful park in the middle of Manhattan. Lionel chose a very tall tree to land in. Pengey balanced on a branch, and Rufus stayed beside him until Lionel had the nest built.

They all slept soundly in the tree in Central Park that night except for Pengey. He was too excited to sleep. Morning couldn't come fast enough, not nearly fast enough.

Chapter 32

A JOURNEY'S END

Morning came as it has for a billion years. The sun rose slowly over the land and the air was light again and the city woke up. Pengey was still awake, and Lionel and Rufus were ready for takeoff.

They huddled together for what might be their last time, for this was the day Rufus would say good-bye to Lionel and Pengey. Rufus said, "I'm not much for words, so I'll just say it was a pleasure to have known you both. I'll miss you, and I hope we see each other again some time."

Lionel sniffed back a tear and said, "Ditto."

Pengey was too choked up to say anything. He started to cry but held back his tears.

Rufus said, "Don't cry. I'm going to miss you Pengey . . . you too, Lionel. And I want you to know I've learned a lot from you both. You're the best friends I could ever have had."

Pengey said, "We all learned a lot, and our friendship will live for ever."

They repeated in chorus, "Our friendship will live forever."

Lionel pointed to a small, nearby lake, and said, "If you ever get down to the city, you can usually find me hanging out around that duck pond."

Rufus looked at Lionel and said, "By the duck pond. If you're ever up around Bar Harbor, up in Maine . . . well, that's where I'll be."

Pengey took the purple ribbon with the silver clasp out of his backpack and placed it over Rufus's neck. "Good-bye, my friend," he said. "We will meet again. I promise."

Rufus just said, "Yes, to be sure."

And with that Rufus lifted off and flew away to find his wife and baby puffin. Off he went, a happy puffin who had made the best friends of his life. They knew that he would be just fine. Lionel and Pengey stood side by side on the branch and waved good-bye until Rufus was long gone from their sight.

Now Pengey and Lionel had their work cut out for them. Pengey reached into his backpack and pulled out Wendy's crumpled business card. He showed it to Lionel, who said, "I don't know how to read, but we can fly around and match up those words with the words on the street signs. My master used to live over on Eighth." He pointed with his wing, "which is that way. So Fifth Avenue has got to be back the other way."

Pengey shrugged his shoulders and said, "I'm so glad you've lived here before."

"Why's that?"

But Pengey was speechless. He just looked around at all the enormous buildings with his beak agape. Then he said in a bewildered tone, "It's so big."

Lionel winked at him and said, "Ah! It ain't so bad after you get used to it. Come on, hop up." Pengey climbed onto Lionel's back. Lionel spread his powerful wings, and they flew off in search of Fifth Avenue.

Now New York is a big city, but there is only one Fifth

Avenue. And it's also true that, while Manhattan Island is extremely tall, it is only a few miles wide. So it only took about an hour to find Wendy's building.

Lionel flew up one side and down the other side of Fifth Avenue. And, sure enough, there on the left side of the street, on a building in the middle of the block, was the number 4380.

Lionel landed and Pengey jumped off. It was a very noisy street with lots of yellow taxicabs and trucks and family cars and motorcycles zooming past and honking their horns.

Lionel looked at Pengey as he jumped off his back and onto the sidewalk. He said, "You sure you want to wait here by yourself?"

Pengey pulled Wendy's business card out of his backpack and said, "This is where it says she lives. You have to find your master. But I'll be here with Wendy if you ever need me."

People passing by on the sidewalk were a little shocked to see a parrot and a penguin standing there, but in New York anything is possible, so no one said anything to either of them.

Pengey took Wendy's red ribbon off Lionel's beak and untied the leather straps from his chest. He put everything away in his backpack. "I guess you won't be needing these any more," said Pengey.

"No, but hold on to them. I'll stop by every once in a while and take you for a ride around the city, okay?"

"Okay."

Pengey took the ribbon and Lionel's aviator wings from his backpack and placed them over Lionel's neck. He said, "I don't know how I can ever thank you."

Lionel held back a tear and said, "Aw, it was nothin', kid." He flapped his wings and was airborne. He flew away and then right back. He hovered there for a minute and said, "I'm going to miss you, kid."

Pengey smiled as only he could smile, and he cooed and waved again, and Lionel took flight to find his master. Now Pengey was all alone on the sidewalks of New York.

Hundreds of people walked by the building. Pengey was so small that most didn't see him at all. People dashed in and out of the building, but the door opened and closed so fast Pengey found it impossible to get inside.

At last a young man walked out. He looked down and saw Pengey. He stooped down and said, "Who do we have here?"

Pengey showed the young man Wendy's business card.

The young man said, "Wendy Fitzgerald. Oh sure man, she's on the twenty-second floor. Just go in there."

He opened the door for Pengey, who politely said, "Thank you very much." Then Pengey trundled into the headquarters of New York City's public television station.

A security guard noticed Pengey and approached him, asking, "Can I help you?"

Pengey showed the security guard Wendy's business card and said in his most humble voice, "Wendy."

The security guard practically passed out. He'd never

heard of a talking penguin, but he looked at the card and handed it back to Pengey. The security guard said, "You have to take the elevator to the twenty-second floor. Right this way."

The guard felt a little strange escorting a ten-inch-tall emperor penguin with a backpack to the elevators, but somehow he knew that this was the right thing to do. He pushed the call button and the elevator doors opened. He got on the elevator with Pengey, and they rode up to the twenty-second floor.

When the doors opened, the security guard pointed and said, "She's right down that hallway. You're all she's talked about since she got back from Antarctica. I don't know how you got here, but it must be a miracle. Go ahead, she's dying to see you."

Pengey walked out into the hall and the security guard called after him, "It's Pengey, Pengey Penguin, right?"

Pengey turned around and looked at the security guard. He bowed most formally and said, "Oui, Monsieur. Pengey J. Penguin."

The elevators closed on a smiling security guard, and Pengey trundled down the hallway to Wendy's office.

Chapter 33

HOME AT LAST

Wendy was sitting at her desk. She looked exceptionally pretty dressed in a light pink sweater and a little plaid skirt. She was busy but she seemed sad.

There was a tap-tap-tap at her door, but it was so faint she thought it must have been her imagination. She walked to her filing cabinet, pulled out a folder, and walked back to her desk.

When her phone rang, she answered it, "Hi, it's Wendy. Oh, hi Jasper. Okay, I'll come down to your office. In about twenty minutes? Sure, no problem."

Wendy pushed a button on her phone and answered another phone call, "Hello. Yes, this is Wendy Fitzgerald. Jean who? Oh! You're a scientist working on a weather ship in the Caribbean. What? You say you saw Pengey? He's on his way to New York in a weather balloon?" Wendy put the phone to her chest and looked at the wall and shook her head in disbelief.

She said to the blank wall in a very dry tone, "This can't be happening."

Jean's voice on the phone sounded very urgent and brought her back to her senses.

Wendy said, "Yes, Jean. I'm still here. Yes, I understand. If he survives the journey he could show up any time.

"Yes, of course, I'll watch the newspapers and monitor the radio and television stations. I'll call the animal shelters. I'll try not to be too anxious, but I've been worried sick about him."

She laughed into the phone, "Yes, I know, he is a little flamboyant. Oh! You nicknamed him 'Monsieur Pengey le Debonair,' did you?"

Wendy laughed again, "Yes, I agree he would look terrific in a top hat and bow tie. Yes of course, you can come and visit him. Any time! Oh? Your ship will be in New York in ten days? Well, I hope to see you then. Of course . . . any friend of Pengey's is a friend of mine. Could you hold the line for a minute? Okay, thanks."

Wendy held the phone and looked perplexed. There was the faint tap-tap-tap at her door again. Then she heard a very small voice say, "Wendy, home?"

It was a tiny voice. She shook her head and thought, "How can this be?" There was the tap-tap-tap again. Wendy got up from her desk and approached her door. She opened it a little and looked out into the hallway. She was looking at people height, so she looked right over Pengey.

Pengey saw her and said, "Wendy . . . Pengey."

Wendy looked down at the floor, and there he was with his little backpack. His feathers were dirty and tattered, but they had grown out to be quite perfect. The yellow orange blush around his cheeks made him look very handsome indeed. He was smiling as only he could smile and cooing as only he could coo and bowing in his most formal fashion.

Wendy picked him up in the palm of her hand and brought him close to her face. She petted his head and kissed his furry little cheek. She held him close and cried tears of joy and happiness.

"How did you ever find me?" she asked. She looked on the floor and saw her battered and torn business card and said, "No, never mind. Don't tell me. Wait, this is impossible. I called the airport in Rio, and they said you had escaped." Tears welled up in her eyes as she said again, "This is absolutely impossible."

Wendy pulled herself together, looked back at her phone, and said to Pengey, "There's someone on the phone for you." Wendy spoke into the phone, "Jean? Are you still there?" She held the receiver up to Pengey's ear.

Jean's voice came over the phone, "Oui, Mademoiselle. I am still here." Pengey looked excited at the sound of Jean's voice.

Wendy pointed to the end of the phone that one talks into and smiled.

Pengey spoke into the phone, "Bonjour, Jean. Pengey home."

Jean's voice came over the phone, "Trés bien, Monsieur Pengey."

"Trés bien, Jean. Pengey home."

Jean said, "Au revoir, Pengey. Au revoir, Wendy."

Wendy said, "Good-bye, Jean."

Wendy hung up the phone and looked into the bright and happy eyes of the littlest penguin. She could still hold him in the palm of her hand. Her eyes glistened with tears of joy that tumbled across her cheeks. She was so happy she thought she was going to burst.

"You're getting to be a handful, you little rascal."

Pengey giggled, "Little rascal."

Wendy smiled and said, "Silly little penguin."

Pengey laughed and said, "Silly little penguin."

Wendy said in her most solemn voice, "This is impossible, you know! This is absolutely impossible."

Pengey just looked at her and smiled as only Pengey could smile and a tear of happiness rolled across his tiny beak.

And Wendy shook her head in disbelief and said, "But you're here, Pengey, you're home."

And so Wendy hugged Pengey lots and lots, and she danced around the room with him.

And Pengey cooed very softly and said with a sigh as soft as a baby's whisper, "Pengey home."

THE END